THE SHORT
HAPPY LIFE OF

MISTER GHICHKA

THE SHORT
HAPPY LIFE OF
MISTER GHICHKA

A   N O V E L

BY

A L A I N   G E R B E R

**Translated by
Jeremy Leggatt**

**Mercury House, Incorporated
San Francisco**

Published in the United States by
Mercury House
San Francisco, California

Distributed to the trade by
Kampmann & Company, Inc.
New York, New York

Manufactured in the United States of America

Library of Congress Cataloging-in-Publication Data

Gerber, Alain, 1943–
  [Heureux jours de monsieur Ghichka.   English]
  The short happy life of Mister Ghichka : a novel / by Alain Gerber ; translated by Jeremy Leggatt.
    p. cm.
  Translation of: Les heureux jours de monsieur Ghichka.
  ISBN 0–916515–35–4 : $14.95
  I. Title.
PQ2667.E674H413   1988
843'.914 – dc 19   87–29497
                                                                        CIP

To Marie José
for a long happy life

" . . . *Man, if he so wishes, can imitate the ape; the ape cannot even wish to imitate man.*"

GEORGES LOUIS LÉCLERC
Count de Buffon
On Degeneration in Animals

Approaching the Crossroads of the Clock that autumn morning, I spied a man who looked like me. "Excuse me, sir, excuse me," I said to him, "but do you recognize me?"

Close up, he was much taller than I was and looked twice as old. And his eyes were very different from mine. They were black; mine are more of a brown-yellow. ("That child wanted to see the world before his time," my grandmother used to say. "It's a bad omen," she would add, smoothing her apron reflectively.)

The thing about this stranger that looked most like me was his cap. I had seen the same cap only the day before yesterday in a window of the Peszczynski Department Store and had said to myself that it was exactly the kind of cap for me to wear in winter. I had even given myself until the following Friday to ask a saleslady its price — thus fighting my natural urge to rush into things.

Although I myself had long since given up chewing tobacco, this man had faint brownish stains at the corners of his mouth. "Good day, Ghichka, how are you?" he said to me. So I stood beside him waiting for the street-car, my heart beating. Perhaps people would take us for old friends. You can never tell what goes on in people's minds.

Inside the streetcar he squeezed over to give me the best seat, the one nearest the window, and handed me a blue ticket. In my confusion I had forgotten to pay for my seat; the stranger had taken care of it. Embarrassed, I thrust my hand deep into my pocket, meaning to repay him immediately. But he stopped my arm with a firm pressure and pointed across the river to the former palace of the dukes of Szpamn. "Look," he said, "the former palace of the dukes of Szpamn."

I looked, and I saw that the north wing of the palace was slightly higher than the west wing. I had looked at this building every morning of my life without once noticing this.

"The architect Wylöhvlo," my neighbor remarked, "was a noted eccentric of his day. He detested symmetry. He maintained that two objects reflecting one another canceled each other out. Duke John ordered his right foot sawed off for his pains."

No one had ever spoken to me in such a learned fashion. People have always assumed that such matters would not interest me. But this man seemed to know me better than many people who had known me all my life.

He also knew our city better than anyone else, and thanks to him I discovered it as if I were seeing it for the very first time. After a short while, I was even grateful to him for telling me the names of familiar places and monuments, for I was seeing them with such new eyes that it was extremely hard for me to identify them. So much so that, when we finally got off the streetcar, I was forced to admit that I had no idea where we were—although that very morning I could have sworn I knew the whole line like the back of my hand.

We walked into a park that sloped gently down to a gleaming lake. It was too early in the season for the trees to have put on their full autumn colors, but you could almost sense them in the varied greens of the foliage. Never before had I been able to focus on such delicate feelings.

"These are the Kirchenstahl Gardens," said my companion, "named for the man who laid them out and introduced the various species of trees and shrubs. A German, I believe. I thought you might like to visit the monkey house."

"Indeed I would," I said.

When I was a little child I used to drag my Aunt Filimor off to the Kirchenstahl Gardens every Sunday to see the monkeys. They were a gift from the crown prince of Bavaria, who happened to be passing through, to the city elders—to make the latter feel at home, or so my father claimed. But we had always turned back at the last moment.

I was so fearful of coming face to face with these animals that I would freeze at the doorway of the red brick building, which was surmounted with the legend "His Highness's Monkey House" in Gothic lettering. I choked on the jungle smells emanating from it; an icy sweat drenched me from head to foot, and I would burst into loud sobs as I implored my aunt to take me home.

And yet, when the big male at the monkey house died three years later after swallowing the doorknob passed to him through the bars by a malevolent prankster, I was stricken with vertigo and forced to take to my bed. I could answer none of the doctor's questions. But I dimly sensed that it would have been pointless to draw his attention to that part of my stomach, in the neighborhood of my navel, that hurt me so much.

Making no attempt to mask his revulsion, the doctor poked and prodded at me from all angles through a sheet. When his examination was over—and I lay broken and racked with pain—he shrugged and recommended rubbing my joints with tincture of arnica.

But I cannot condemn him: How could he have guessed that I was suffering another's pain? A monkey's pain, what was more—and a monkey on which I had never even laid eyes.

"He's going to recover, isn't he?" I heard my sister ask disappointedly as she helped him on with his fur coat in the corridor.

"Temporarily—like all the rest of us" was the doctor's terse reply as he took leave of my mother at the front door.

For the next three days, hands pressed fiercely on my navel, I could only weep.

To console me, my aunt brought over a collection of postcards showing the deceased monkey in a whole series of costumes, situations, and postures. I refused even to glance at them, screwing my eyes so tightly shut that multicolored stars exploded inside my head.

But while my father was at work and my mother was outside talking to a neighbor, my sister stole into my room, pulled a chair up to my bed, and, with her mouth to my ear, began to describe the cards one by one in a whisper.

In one picture, the monkey was smoking a pipe, a streetcar driver's cap perched on the side of his head. In another he was arrayed in maid's cap and apron and held a silver tray laden with steaming cups arranged around a dish of pastries. In a third he was combing his hair in a pier mirror with an enormous comb. Or else he was a mailman, handing out mail at the new municipal post office to real mailmen collapsing with mirth. As the appalling series continued, he poured glasses of beer; rode a bicycle; walked attired as a bridegroom with his bride on his arm; played cards; stood sentry; posed in baffled contemplation of a bust of the lexicographer Littré; snuffed out a candle; fished for carp in a tank.

Paralyzed with horror, legs awash in urine, I listened to my sister's merciless monotone as she outlined these depravities, the smallest detail of which was agony to me. This went on until I sank into unconsciousness.

Much later, after a fortuitous event (I mean the dairy truck that seemed to veer deliberately off its path to flatten her — my sister — like a pancake against the wall of the Kursaal), I was to find that she had taken advantage of my tight-shut eyes to invent the final stroke that had robbed me of my senses on that far-off day. I was going through her things after our return from the funeral when I found those same cards, yellowed with age, in an envelope inscribed in a fine angular hand "Proof of My Brother's Stupidity — March 16, 1925." In none of the pictures, numbered one to twelve, could I find what she had described to me that day — namely, a picture of the poor beast sucking on two doorknobs emerging from a double ice-cream cone.

I was twenty-three when my sister fell victim to the dairy truck. By that time I was no longer, properly speaking, afraid of monkeys — provided, of course, that they were not adult gorillas, notorious for their uncertain temper and hideous savagery.

But I confess that I did not seek them out. In truth, you would have had to pay me dearly to hazard such an encounter with the unknown and cross the malodorous threshold of His Highness's Monkey House, where the prince's baboons had mysteriously died one after the other and been replaced—according to the newspapers—by representatives of a coarser but more durable species.

I have no idea what power the man with black eyes exercised over me, but I followed him into the monkeys' lair without a twinge of fear. At most, I experienced a kind of heaviness at navel level, a symptom I attributed to the two extra slices of toast I had wolfed down that morning almost without bothering to chew.

In any case, there was no call whatsoever for concern. With the exception of a solitary, stubborn-visaged primate pacing up and down behind the bars as if he imagined that his determined gait might actually take him somewhere, the animals were all lying about on the ground, to all appearances fast asleep.

The man with me—he had insisted on paying for both of us when we had entered the red brick building, arguing that it had been his idea to visit the monkeys—pointed at the pacing animal and declared, "The others are nothing but a pack of idlers, but Karl there is always on the qui vive. He wouldn't stoop to snoozing in public, would you, Karl?"

The animal he had addressed continued his vigilant patrolling, but now he threw us an intrigued look over his shoulder. My companion nudged me discreetly and warned me to watch for what happened next.

"Karl is a highly conscientious monkey," he said in penetrating tones as the animal reached the wall and mechanically turned in his tracks. "He earns his keep! He's at the public's beck and call from crack of dawn till closing time. Isn't that so, Karl?"

The monkey appeared to be weighing these flattering words, his gaze now directed unwaveringly at my companion. When he reached the spot where we stood, he stopped, turned toward us, raised two fingers to the peak of an invisible cap, and stood clasping the bars in his hands, exactly like a man at a ticket window waiting to answer your questions.

"Aha!" cried the man with the black eyes, delighted with this strange behavior. "Karl at your service, eh? What did I tell you? Wonderful, old friend, wonderful!"

There was now a gleam of vanity in the monkey's eyes. Puffing out his chest, he smiled smugly and hopped from one foot to the other.

"Karl," the man went on, "may I introduce Mister Ghichka, who is both a man of honor and a friend? Much more than a friend . . . "

My throat tightened at this praise, but the monkey seemed unimpressed. Glancing briefly at me, he gave a casual nod.

"Do you know what Mister Ghichka does for a living?" my companion asked with an eagerness I found difficult to understand.

Eyes half-closed, a thoughtful hand scratching his chin, Karl inspected me.

"You don't know," my companion cackled. "You'll never get it!"

I looked at the man in amazement, but he was too jubilant even to notice my existence.

Karl, on the other hand, was frowning harder than ever and had stuck his head through the bars to stare right into my eyes. I could feel his stinking breath against my face. He stretched his muzzle — is "muzzle" the right word? — into a thoughtful grimace, exposing his big yellow teeth and dark gums. Finally his jaws began to move as if he were mumbling to himself. He was trying to hide it, but I could see that he was angry with me.

"Mister Ghichka is an accounting clerk!" roared my companion in unabashed triumph. (I scarcely recognized in him the irreproachably proper individual I had met but a short while before at the Crossroads of the Clock. You would have thought it was the first time he had ever had the opportunity to give such hilarious information to a monkey. To Karl's clear annoyance, tears of joy were streaming down his cheeks.) "An accounting clerk, my friend!" he repeated. "What do you think of that?"

For a moment the monkey considered me with suspicion, hoping perhaps that I would deny it. Then, shrugging resignedly, he shambled toward a small iron door at the back of the cage.

To reach it he was obliged to step over the inert bodies of several of his fellows. Standing beside me, the man I had met that morning was guffawing like a buffoon and dabbing at his eyes with an embroidered handkerchief.

I watched him out of the corner of my eye, amazed.

By now, I was certain that we bore not the slightest physical or moral resemblance to one another. In fact, it would have been hard to unearth two more utterly different people in the whole town. I would have left him then and there had I dared. I suddenly thought of my puzzled colleagues, eyeing my empty desk above their busily scratching pens. In my mind's eye I saw assistant manager Krokody, pale, embittered, fuming inwardly over the scandal of my unexplained absence . . .

In front of me, Karl had pushed through the little door and disappeared into the darkness of a small room where we could hear him bustling mysteriously about.

It seemed too much for my companion.

"Oh, Lord!" he groaned unbelievingly, his expression one of almost painful ecstasy.

He literally choked when the monkey reappeared, threading his way with difficulty through the sleepers and hauling a large wooden table. Panting, he set it down on the other side of the bars, facing me.

Whereupon—after pausing to catch his breath and look reproachfully at me—he went back to the iron door, followed by the black-eyed man's helpless laughter.

This time, Karl returned with a chair, which he set before the table without paying us the slightest attention.

"Look how angry he is!" spluttered my companion, almost sobbing with mirth. "Isn't that so, Karl?"

The animal proceeded as if he had heard nothing. My neighbor, his face crimson and streaked with sweat, threw his head back, eyes closed, mouth wide open, as he fought to control the convulsions that shook him. Squeezing his chest between both hands, he sucked in the fetid air around us with the desperate greed of a drowning man.

But here came the monkey again, burdened with books and ledgers. He set them down carefully on the table in what was obviously a premeditated order and then, extending his monstrous lips in an extravagant pout, blew a thick layer of dust off these articles and full into our faces.

At once, my companion's tongue and eyes protruded violently from his head and he bent double, while I administered hearty slaps to his shoulder blades. With unshaken dignity, Karl returned to the back of his cage.

When I looked up again a few moments later — the man beside me had survived his choking fit by a hair — our monkey was once more standing at the table. On it he had set a heavy cut-glass inkwell with a silver stopper and a pale wooden pen case, the image of the pen case I myself had been using these past eight years and five months — a last gift from my poor sister.

He raised the stopper and slid the lid off the pen case, extracting from it a tapered pen, its fattest third painted black and the rest red. Closing one eye, he meticulously checked the gap at the tip of the nib. (I recognized it immediately, an Amiral No. 5, the make I had always preferred.)

He dipped it in the inkwell. Shook it deftly as he withdrew it from the orifice. Made a few exploratory doodles on a sheet of rough paper he had taken from a ledger. Gauged the result of this initial test, cocking his head first left, then right. Repeated the experiment, and finally gave a grunt that could have passed for a cough of satisfaction.

To avoid following the animal's movements, my companion had buried his face in his hands, but soon he was furtively watching the scene through his fingers and beginning to shake again from shoulders to ankles. The monkey flashed him an irritated glare before turning his back on us once more and moving off with a heavy rolling gait.

"My God!" the man wheezed helplessly. "My God!"

I sensed that I should have taken advantage of his condition to escape and fly to the chambers of Morchiev, Morchiev & Sons while I still had a chance of getting myself out of the mess I was in with minimum damage: a warning from Mister Krokody, perhaps a few strokes of his cane, and a substantial cut in wages . . . But I was rooted to the spot by the absurd compulsion to witness the monkey's act — even though I could already tell that it would wound me to the depths of my soul.

Fascinated, I went on gazing at the metal door through which the primate had once again disappeared. Beside me, trembling violently, the black-eyed man was uttering little involuntary whimpers, like a puppy. Together we waited — he in a state of morbid excitement, I in a kind of resigned horror.

Just what was the stupid monkey up to?

Was it possible that he had retired into the bowels of some suffocating lair, leaving us standing out here like fairground oafs, vacuously contemplating an empty chair and a table capriciously strewn with the tools of the accounting clerk's trade?

It seemed as if he had been gone for hours. But a glance at my watch reassured me. I was the dupe of my own impatience: It had been a mere ten minutes since we had entered His Highness's Monkey House.

And there he was again.

Good heavens, what was he wearing?

He had fastened a stiff collar under his chin; from it hung a broad ivory dickey vertically bisected by a somber outmoded cravat. Over it he wore a gray smock that flapped about his heels, its arms sheathed from wrist to elbow in sateen oversleeves. A black cloth skullcap, pulled down to the eyebrows, completed his garb.

I distinctly heard the grinding of my companion's teeth: Unable to take any more, he was battling to strangle a renewed assault of mirth.

Looking ill-tempered and absorbed, Karl drew near. Perching himself on the chair, he opened a huge double-entry ledger, dipped the tip of his Amiral No. 5 in the inkwell, and, referring as the need arose to a variety of notebooks, registers, ledgers, and stub books, set about completing a half-finished page. The tip of his tongue, peeping out through his lips, looked obscenely pink to me.

Curious sounds — gargling, spluttering, strangled belches, the spitting of a frying pan — were reaching me from my companion, but they seemed mere echoes of phenomena occurring miles away. I was aware of them as if through a dense fog. They lapped at the threshold of my consciousness but did not cross it. For every ounce of my attention was being sucked in by the monkey's mimicry, his gestures, the smallest twitch of his eyebrows.

Gradually my mind perceived, and then accepted as irrefutable fact, the notion that I was face to face not just with an animal trained to reproduce the exact gestures and attitudes that were mine ten hours a day, six days a week, but, even more, with a picture of myself as faithful as my own reflection in a mirror.

I caught myself sticking my own tongue out of the corner of my mouth and penning phantom words and figures in a nonexistent ledger on an imaginary table. I have no idea whose will was governing my movements, but there it was: Whenever the monkey leaned forward, I leaned forward; whenever he plunged his nib in the inkwell, I thrust my hand forward and dipped thumb, index, and middle finger, clustered about a fictitious pen, into the void; whenever he sighed and raised his gaze to the ceiling, I sighed and raised my gaze to the ceiling—to feel instant apprehension lest Mister Krokody intercept my look and detect in it a mark of disloyalty to the firm of Morchiev, Morchiev & Sons.

In fact, so strikingly synchronized were Karl's gestures and my own that it would have been impossible to say who was imitating whom.

It was more as if we possessed but one brain, but one spinal column. Was I in him? Was he in me? Was I watching him? Or was I not observing myself through the eyes of the primate? Who was in the cage? Who was at liberty?

And what if, for more than eight years, I had been drawing a modest pittance, not to put order into the accounts of Morchiev, Morchiev & Sons, but to ape, in a small dusty room under the ferule of a brutal turnkey and surrounded by beings blighted by the same destiny as my own, the grimaces and mannerisms of a monkey in the Kirchenstahl Gardens?

Abruptly, as if it had burned my fingers, I dropped the implement my hand had believed it was holding and stared at the creature opposite me with unspeakable horror.

And at that precise moment, the red and black penholder rolled from Karl's grasp, leaving a hideous inkblot on the ledger, as the monkey leaned back in his chair and stared at me with eyes suddenly grown huge.

For a long time we locked gazes, our mouths twitching involuntarily. Then Karl rolled off his seat and with a piercing scream fled toward the iron door.

As for me, before I even realized what was happening, I found myself flat on my face on a small stone bench outside the building, sobbing shamelessly into my hands.

I could feel a small crowd gathering around me, but the voice of the man I had so unluckily met that morning cut in with unexpected firmness to disperse the onlookers who—to judge from their dragging footsteps—were most reluctant to leave the scene.

The man sat next to me and put a fatherly arm around my shoulders.

"Come, come!" he murmured, his voice low and warm. "He's just an animal whose capacity for mimicry has been systematically developed through endless repetition. He meant no disrespect, I swear it! He was just doing what he's been taught to do, that's all! Come on, Ghichka, please don't take it so much to heart. You're not going to let a monkey get your goat, are you?" And, as I continued to blubber out my despair, "Ghichka, pull yourself together! You take yourself too seriously, my boy. Just think! An accounting clerk isn't even Karl's best act. You should see him do a surrealist, for example, or a sewer worker! They're really something to write home about, believe me! Can you hear me, Ghichka? Don't take it so hard! Listen, Ghichka, I'll tell you what we're going to do. We're going to go back in there . . . " (I shook my head violently and sobbed anew.) "Will you listen to me? You don't even know what I'm going to say! We'll go back to Karl—I'll pay—and we'll ask him, just for you, to do the act most experts consider his finest: the stamp collector."

"No!" I squealed. "For pity's sake!"

"Just wait!" he cooed insistently. "You won't believe your eyes! By the end of his act the stamp album is in shreds, and he's covered in stamps from the tip of his tail to the top of his skull. What do you think of that, eh? Good Lord, Ghichka, it's not something you're ever likely to see again. But perhaps you'd prefer him to do a monkey swallowing a doorknob he's mistaken for an egg . . . ?"

I heard no more. For the second time in my life, I lost consciousness.

I came to my senses in a room that was strangely familiar. By that I mean that at first glance it looked very
much like my own room, except that nothing in it was
exactly the same.

You might say that there was the same vague similarity
between the two places as there was between the stranger
of the Crossroads of the Clock and myself.

And who but that same stranger was sitting beside the
sofa on which I lay? He smiled at me most gently.

"You are at home here," he said to me.

But it was a singularly ambiguous remark. I did not
know exactly how to interpret it. Did he mean — and if he
did, how arrogant he was! — that I was back at my lodg-
ings in Astraghy Street (snugly settled in my sister's old
room with its wallpaper of marquises in swings)? Or was
he intimating, in a paroxysm of tact, that I could consider his home my own? I dared not ask. But there was
one point that needed clarification.

"I have telephoned Morchiev, Morchiev & Sons to

inform them of your condition, my dear Ghichka," he said with an affectionate smile.

I sat up abruptly, the blood ebbing from my head to my heart.

"Good God, what condition?"

"A certain Mister Kokodry brought you this," he went on, ignoring my question.

"Krokody," I corrected him mechanically, staring in amazement at the enormous bunch of lilies and box of chocolates (it must have weighed at least five pounds) sitting on the table in the middle of the room.

The man blushed.

"And this is from me," he murmured, his gaze lowered, as he handed me a package he had been hiding behind his back.

"It is nothing, really!" he stammered as I struggled to untie the gold cord.

Inside the elegant wrapping was the cap I had so admired in the window of the Peszczynski Department Store. Just as I feared, it was a little too big, falling to my nostrils and making it difficult for me to see. It would certainly have suited my benefactor better—what a pity he already possessed one.

"They told me it would be perfectly convenient to exchange it if it didn't fit . . . ," he went on with a shy smile.

I waved my hands in the air.

"No, no! It's fine. It's just right. Absolutely perfect. Perhaps a little cotton wool inside the brim . . . It's splendid! I've been dreaming about it for so long!"

"I know," he replied, blushing to the roots of his hair. Then, to cover his confusion, "Ah, yes, I mustn't forget. Old Zbylo Morchiev has decided to raise your salary. And because of your condition he has granted you a year's leave of absence."

Just beside me was a small window whose yellow and orange lozenge-shaped panes were fitted together with strips of lead.

Through this benign filter I gazed out at the street.

From its appearance and from the number of passersby, I judged it to be around six in the evening. Perhaps six-fifteen. The shadows were lengthening and certain details were losing their sharpness. It would not be long before the light faded.

A delicious numbness stole over me. All my old fears, all my unrequited desires were at rest. Soon my eyes would close, and I would drift out on an ocean as slow and as gentle as smoke. Outside, the passersby were quickening their steps. The dark hues of the rooftops began to slide down into the streets. Suddenly, quite unexpectedly, the first snow of the year was settling on the town.

But I was already walking in my dreams across the gentle swell of the wheat fields.

The half-year I spent behind that window or behind others very much like it in that snug apartment in the Kristophory quarter was the happiest time of my whole life. And the only time that ever brought me a sense of completeness.

I cannot say whether my condition improved or worsened, never having had (and still not having) a very precise grasp of what afflicted me. But I can say without fear of contradiction that I had never felt better within my own body and that, after a few months, I even achieved what had been denied me at birth and what had become more and more elusive through my youth — peace of mind.

Was it from contemplating the world through that summer-hued window? It suddenly seemed more luminous, more welcoming. And less precarious. It would last forever, bravely telling off the seasons thousands by thousands; and everything in it, the smallest speck of dust on the sidewalk opposite, the most delicate snowflake bobbing above the basilica's bulbous spire, everything in it took on tremendous importance for me. I imagined that the universe held infinite possibilities of love and joy hidden within its every particle. That thought alone was enough to fill me with love and joy.

From October to March I gazed out on delicate, fragile dusks, mere mists. For hours on end I watched children sliding along roadways frozen into skating rinks at Christmastime. And, when I ventured to open the window on New Year's morning, it came to me in a kind of illumination that the snow was not white but pink, blue, and violet, the color of countless scents no one had ever managed to bottle. I immediately pulled the window shut, my heart beating wildly: The beauty of the earth is sometimes so violent that you should sample it in small doses lest it prove too strong for your heart.

Until then I had never savored the days. I had moved through the different stages of my life without beginning to suspect their overpowering splendor, a splendor that makes you at once smaller and bigger, that makes you the right size for the size of the earth.

I had not stopped to look at things, for I had been unaware that each thing summarizes all others. I had not stopped to look at myself. I had imagined myself to be like other people, like monkeys, like assistant manager Krokody (within reason, of course), like my sister who had hated me even as I had worshiped her countenance and the lock of fair hair I had picked up at the barber's and daily persuaded myself was hers.

That was what my life had been. No life at all, as you can see. Not even anything that had truly belonged to me.

For my life had belonged to the obstinacy of my mother who, while still a girl, had dreamed of a son with flashing teeth whom she could flaunt before less fortunate neighbors and lead to the altar in dragoon's uniform when summer came.

It had belonged to the indifference of my father, a simple, self-satisfied man, who opened his mouth only to drain his beer glass or to utter inanities.

It had belonged to the hostility of my sister, as implacable as it was incomprehensible.

And to the loud disparaging remarks made about me by a great many people who appeared to be inconvenienced by the simple fact of my existence.

And to the biased attitude of my schoolmaster who, incapable of grasping that I was not quite the oaf he had taken me for at first glance, would salute my rare triumphs with even heavier irony than he would the mournful parade of my failures.

And to the unremitting vindictiveness of Infantry Sergeant Major Bruhnka who, in the wreckage of his declining years (or so I am told), daily salutes with his left hand the bottle of formaldehyde in which his right arm is preserved.

And to Mister Krokody's venomous expression, to his immaculate cuffs, to his fearsome pince-nez.

To old Zbylo Morchiev's avarice.

To the jeers of the beggar to whom I give alms every Sunday outside Saint Barnabas and All Saints.

To the scathing laughter of Maria Wakhelyana, whom in my innocence I had tried to woo and who considered herself too beautiful even to tell me no.

To the insolence of butcher's apprentice Yagel Naftali,

21

who treated me even more cavalierly than he treated his employer.

To the scoffing of streetcar crewmen as I ran and stumbled in pursuit of the streetcar.

To the thousands of glances from the thousands of people who were ashamed of me for reasons that forever remained obscure to me . . .

But that nightmare was over. Gradually, through a succession of delectable meditations, I was reclaiming my life and myself.

The man whose guest I was supported me through this exhilarating process. Who was he? What did it matter since, thanks to him, I was myself? Why had I accosted him in the first place? What did it matter since, thanks to him, I had finally accosted myself? Where did he know me from? What did it matter since, thanks to him, I knew myself at last? He was a man who took care of me, that was all.

We breakfasted across from one another at the kitchen table, taking pleasure in conversing with our eyes as we sipped our scalding coffee. Then he would leave me; not once did I feel the need to ask him where he was going.

At five he came home. He rarely failed to bring me a present.

Once it was colored crayons. Another day, a yo-yo. Or a top. Trifles, so as not to embarrass me. A wooden whistle. A photo of a naked woman: You lifted her buttocks and there were the mass graves of Verdun. A flower-embroidered proverb: "Why should I beat myself? My wife will take care of that!" or else "A rolling stone gathers no moss."

He was a man who liked to laugh.

I should have gathered that from his behavior in the Kirchenstahl Gardens as we stood watching Karl's antics. But at that time I was a fearful young man with no sense of my own being, for whom all of life's events were an occasion for terror and humiliation, and who seized the slightest excuse for self-pity, living as if the world were a bed of nails on which his tortured body was forced to lie.

Yet I did not regret having been such a person. How otherwise could I have sunk to the state that had led me first to shelter and then to self-revelation at the hands of this extraordinary person?

He never made the slightest allusion to my stupid conduct that day. On the other hand, he spoke to me often of Karl, masking his deep affection for the monkey behind mocking and even outright sarcastic remarks. But I was not fooled: From the moisture in his eye, the tender curve of his lip, from the dreamy expression that brushed across his visage like the shadow of a wing every time he mentioned the animal (which was often), you could tell that he admired and loved him more than he cared to admit.

I treated this predilection of his with the greatest understanding, even though I found it excessive. I believe I even encouraged it, but, since I, too, was reserved in my own way, I pretended to take it all very lightly.

I must admit that at first (before I accomplished the transformation that would free my true self from its prison of anxieties), I could not help betraying my extreme distaste whenever he mentioned the monkey and his exploits. In fact, I would turn pale and avert my gaze.

Right up to the middle of November, I remained unable to banish from my mind the notion that I was no more or less than the human facsimile of the animal. Secretly I cursed him (which, of course, merely served to make myself more contemptible in my own eyes).

But one fine day, musing by the window, awaiting my host's return and wondering what he might be bringing me, my error was revealed to me in a flash; I instantly ceased to perceive the slightest resemblance between Karl and myself, any more than I could detect a resemblance between the person I had thought I was and the person I really was (that is, the person I was about to become).

As if he had sensed the revolution that had taken place inside me while he was out and about in town, my benefactor appeared, his face aglow with happiness, carrying a box of sugared almonds, a bottle of sparkling wine, and a recalcitrant lobster, which we were obliged to pursue under the furniture on all fours before we could plunge it into the pot of boiling water that awaited it.

I would have shouted aloud that this was the most beautiful day of my life if the revelation of the true Ghichka, this handsome stranger, had not been accompanied by another revelation — that of the incomparable and equal beauty of every second we spend on earth once we have discovered the love within us.

I literally devoured my share of the lobster. It was exquisite; in a way it reminded me of the salmon fritters my grandmother Khoprühlka, whose resourcefulness was legendary, used to make from breadcrumbs soaked in a can of sardines.

For some time, my companion had been holding his sides. Tears of laughter were welling up in his eyes and splashing clear across to the edge of my plate. When he had calmed down a little, he asked me whether I would not have preferred eating the lobster without its shell. I was horribly embarrassed, but he quickly assured me that my inexperience excused my error.

It was also the first time I had tasted sparkling wine. It turned my head a little. I played the fool. I recited the comic monologue that had earned my father such a big hand at weddings. (Until that moment I had not realized that I remembered it so well, but I swear that I recalled it down to the last belly rumble and faithfully reproduced the bride's farts, which were without doubt the high point of the act.)

Warming to my role, I hoisted a chair in the air with my arms held rigid before me. I ripped the Persian rug into three pieces doing a wild Muscovite fling. I rushed to get the horsehair broom from the closet in the kitchen, but by the time I came panting back I had forgotten what I had intended to do with the implement.

My host was in seventh heaven.

Even the mutilation of his Oriental rug had merely triggered anew the delightful asphyxiation of uncontrollable mirth. He brayed, he shuddered, he stretched imploring arms toward me, begging me at once to put an end to his misery and to dream up some fresh clownery.

When I had to open the window in order to vomit, he fell from his chair so heavily that the lamp almost detached itself from the ceiling.

I watched him from under my armpit as I went on relieving my system. Never had I felt such deep emotion at the simple idea that there was someone by my side. I had to restrain myself from going over and embracing him.

Instead, I carefully wiped my lips. I closed the window, for it was a frosty, bitingly cold night. Gradually my host collected himself, his gaze suddenly solemn, and I felt myself grow solemn in turn.

Our eyes met: I was standing by the window, while he was still on all fours by the grandfather clock whose pendulum swung in a strangely passionless rhythm; we remained rooted in these positions until dawn, I believe; we stayed there until something familiar and compassionate took us gently by the shoulders and steered us toward our bedrooms with a patience and a kindness that do not exist in ordinary life—because there should be nothing ordinary in a life.

Next day was a Sunday. For dinner we polished off the sparkling wine with a can of peas.

The man cleared his throat. In a low voice, without looking at me, he began to talk about his feelings for Karl.

I listened attentively, my eyes full of tears. Not only did I understand the subtlest shades of the emotions he was describing, but I discovered that they found an echo in my own spirit.

In other words, I began to fall in love with the monkey. Realizing this, I congratulated myself for not carrying out my project.

An idea had come to me as I was getting up that morning: To entertain my benefactor and to demonstrate to him that I was now free of my fetters, I would give him a performance of Karl miming the antics of an accounting clerk. Only the practical obstacles in the way of such a project had deterred me. (Where and how to procure cuff protectors on a Sunday afternoon? And, above all, what artifices to exploit in order to show plainly that I was imitating the monkey and not the accounting clerk—which would have been of little interest?)

I was now most grateful to circumstances for forestalling my plan. I do not believe that my companion, infatuated as he was with this animal, would have relished the masquerade; moreover, such deep affection for the monkey was now welling up inside me that I would almost certainly have died of shame had I compromised him, even indirectly, in such a deplorable display.

Having discovered the infinite resources and elusive subtleties of the heart, I was amazed.

"Is it possible," I asked myself, "that Maria Wakhelyana, whose whole body is a hymn to tenderness and bliss, could be so dim of soul as to be unaware of the existence of all this? How can human beings, so deprived of everything else, be ignorant of the enormous wealth waiting to be mined in their own bosoms?"

But I, too, had been like them. Just the day before—before that instant of pure ecstasy in which truth had been revealed to me in one stroke—I had paid no heed to the imperceptible stirrings of my being. My heart had given me terrible pain, yet I had not listened to it. I had ordered my heart to be dumb. I had listened to external sounds, just like cavemen huddled fearfully together through the long, roaring, growling nights. And the world had been all threat, ageless and deadly, oh, Maria Wakhelyana! I had not known it. I had not yet been born to myself.

The first time I ventured outside the cocoon of my

friend's apartment (I could call him my friend now) was to visit Karl at His Highness's Monkey House.

Winter was drawing to a close as precociously and as suddenly as it had begun. Nature was a good month ahead of the calendar. When you reached the bottom of the Street of the Blessed Pontiffs, which is one of the longest streets in our city, taking you directly from the Kristophory quarter to the Gunpowderworks in the heart of old Krazkoch, you realized that the sun, although pale and watery against a cloudless sky of palest blue, gave off the kind of heat you normally do not expect until Easter.

On Jübhal Jabhü Street a young woman pensively walking her dog had opened a yellow parasol. Freshly cleaned windowpanes glittered from the facades of houses, always a sure sign of the rekindling of human hopes.

From the Gunpowderworks we walked to the Carousel, and then along the interminable wall of the former Imperial Guards' barracks, topped with broken bottle ends, as far as the Kirchenstahl Gardens. It was quite a walk, but the air was so sparkling and the buildings so splendid under the pristine sun . . .

Although it was Sunday the park was almost deserted, and there was not a mouse stirring in the red brick building. Karl was pacing behind his bars. The other monkeys were sleeping like logs: You would have sworn they had not moved a muscle since that fateful September day when I had come here for the first time.

My friend and I congratulated Karl warmly for his vigilance and for his dedication to exercise, which keeps the body fit and promotes a harmonious circulation in the brain.

He listened to us, leaning nonchalantly against the bars and nodding whenever we made a point with which he concurred. Very soon I had forgotten that the Creator had not endowed him with the gift of speech. It was exactly as if I were chatting with an old chum.

As a result, I was reluctant to manipulate him for our amusement, and I sensed that my companion felt likewise. But it was the animal who, without our making the slightest request, motioned us to be patient and went over to the iron door.

He returned almost immediately, sporting a straw hat and malacca cane.

Turning in profile to us, he gazed at a point straight in front of him and began to speak (I mean, to imitate someone speaking). His expression reflected such real distress, helplessness, and despair that we felt no desire whatsoever to laugh (and, besides, we had been unable to identify any particular person in his mime).

Karl explained something to his invisible interlocutor. He made a gesture of stuffing food into his mouth, shaped the outline of something bulky with his hands, pushed his hat back on his head, and pretended to pull bank notes from his wallet and count them over and over again. Then he sighed ponderously, let his arms fall to his sides, and despondently shook his head.

My friend and I looked at each other. What was it all about? We had not the slightest idea. But there had been something pathetic and heartrending in the riddle.

Next the monkey set the hat on the ground, relinquished his cane, and moved across to the exact spot he had been addressing while still burdened with these props. His shoulders drooped (his fingertips trailing to his heels), his chin dropped dolefully to his chest, and he assumed a striking likeness to a sad monkey. It was mesmerizing, and I felt a hot tide of tears rise to my eyes at this spectacle of distress. On my right, my companion was already racked with sobs.

But I cannot claim that either of us had grasped the inner meaning of this sorrowful scene — except that it involved an elegant, distressed gentleman talking to a horribly unhappy monkey about matters related in some way to money, to food, and to a mysterious object possessing the same rough dimensions as a Bavarian clothes cupboard.

I was puzzling over it, and my companion, having wiped his eyes, was doing the same. But nothing came. Karl was forced to begin his act all over again, exaggerating each effect in order to make it more understandable.

Just then, my attention was distracted by a sense of a fourth presence in the building.

I turned, and jumped so suddenly that my friend, startled by this unexpected reaction, was unable to hold back a cry of fear. Behind us, silhouetted against the open doorway, Karl was watching us! I confess to a feeling of panic as he approached, straw hat at a slightly rakish angle, cane lightly tapping his leg in time with his steps.

Then the light fell on his face, and I realized with relief that the newcomer, although boasting a hat and cane identical to those in Karl's possession, was a man and not a monkey. In fact (as he himself was about to inform us), he was the zoo director.

"Gentlemen," he said to us after we had introduced ourselves (he was smiling politely, but you could tell his heart was not in it), "I sense in you the representatives of a rare breed: true monkey-lovers. More than that (forgive me!)—connoisseurs, specialists, experts . . . "

He waited hopefully for us to confirm his supposition.

"Well," stammered my friend with a blush, "in all modesty I had thought that to be the case . . . until this afternoon, that is . . . "

The director frowned but did his best to conceal his disappointment.

"This afternoon?"

"A minute ago. Just now! Neither Mister Ghichka nor I have any idea what Karl is getting at. It is the first time this has happened, I assure you, but . . . "

He stopped, too upset to go on.

The director shot the briefest of glances at the monkey, who had retrieved his hat and cane and was standing on the other side of the bars in a posture faithfully mirroring that of the man we were speaking to.

"Ah," the latter said gravely. "He was miming the interview we had together this very morning. You could not have guessed it."

"About money, was it not?" broke in my companion, anxious to redeem himself a little.

The director's face brightened.

"That is so."

"And about food?"

"Exactly. You did understand, you see!"

"But . . . ," I interrupted, raising a timid forefinger, "the Bavarian clothes cupboard?"

The man's face crumpled. He paled and stared at me, then at Karl, then back at me, his expression one of surprise mingled with anxiety, even terror.

"The . . . Bavarian cupboard?" he croaked tonelessly.

"Yes," I said, "you know what I mean."

And, as well as I was able, I repeated the gesture I had twice seen the monkey make.

Visibly reassured, the official burst into hearty laughter, the primate at once following suit.

"Oh, that? It was his way of conveying the idea of an 'enormous quantity.' An enormous quantity of food—that was exactly the subject of our discussion this morning."

As we stared at him uncomprehendingly, clearly waiting to be told more, he cast a look around us to make sure we were absolutely alone, then beckoned us closer. He was not satisfied until our heads were touching his. Karl, in turn, thrust his head through the bars so that we formed a conspiratorial square, cheek to cheek.

"Gentlemen," whispered the director, continuing to dart vigilant glances over his shoulder, "what I am about to tell you is extremely serious and must remain between us."

My friend, the monkey, and I readily acquiesced. The director's voice went down an octave.

"The municipality has decided to tighten its budget. To do this it has targeted, as it must, all money-losing operations. By a tragic coincidence, his highness's dear monkey house is one of these. Presiding as I do over its fortunes, I refuse to lay the responsibility for this failure on any other than your obedient servant. But, as you will readily agree, the great majority of our fellow citizens are not monkey-lovers. Far from it! In fact, I would venture that they feel toward monkeys such marked and stubborn indifference that it shatters all statistical laws—indeed, borders on the pathological!"

Once again we agreed.

"To be brief, although we possess in Karl a specimen (and I do not hesitate to declare it in his presence, at whatever risk to his modesty) that I would confidently pronounce exceptional, our takings for a whole year do not begin to cover outgoings for a single week's bananas, peanuts, and Turkish cigarettes."

Karl confirmed this claim with energetic nods, which the director acknowledged with a small tilt of his head before going on, "This establishment, gentlemen, is largely my own creation, but I may be frank with you: I will not be sorry to see it disappear. I do all I can. I sink three-quarters of my salary into it—ask my poor daughters, obliged to wear dresses three years out of date to the garrison ball and heaped with irreparable insults in consequence—but bad luck has dogged me. Prices are soaring, particularly for bananas, of which Karl (like all members of his species) is inordinately fond." (With a jerk of his thumb, the monkey drew our attention to a corner of his cage: There, indeed, was a three-foot heap of banana peels.) "The price of electricity has almost doubled since last year. The bonuses extorted from me on the slightest pretext by the fat sow knitting behind the ticket window would be enough to feed a pair of orangutans for six months! And the worst thing is, she has clout with the municipality! 'A case of social need,' they say. The truth is, she's a degenerate who stuffs her ill-gotten gains into a washbasin and ecstatically dunks her fat backside in it whenever the moon changes! But what can I do? Everyone is against me! With our last mayor, I was at least able to defend my point of view, but this new one is a notorious primatophobe. I know very well that he has but one idea in his head—to transform this animal enclosure into an open-air restaurant."

"An open-air restaurant!" we cried with one voice, my companion and I. "And Karl?"

"Karl?" The director, suddenly gloomy, was smiling a painfully twisted smile. "We shall have to shoot him."

As we started in horror, our hair standing straight up from our scalps, the monkey moved back a pace or two, closed one eye, raised an object we had no trouble identifying to his cheek, and pretended to shoot.

"But," moaned my companion, "what about the others? Every one of them is bone idle, a useless mouth . . . "

"The others?" The light of madness kindled briefly in the official's eyes, to be extinguished almost immediately, leaving behind what looked like dying embers in the depths of his gaze. "The others went down that road a long time ago, my dear sir! Sacrificed one by one—and on my orders!—in the insane hope of saving at least one, my dear old Karl!" A tear appeared in the corner of his eye. His voice cracked. "You think they are asleep, do you not? Well, you are right, they are asleep. Eternally asleep. What you see there are their poor remains, crudely sewn around bundles of rags!"

As if to corroborate his words, Karl went over to the nearest of the inert forms and with a masterful kick sent it soaring to the rafters. When it fell back to earth he seized one of its hands and gripped it solemnly, reflectively shaking the arm that hung limply over the shapeless heap that was the rest of the doll.

It was too much for the director, who began to blubber like a schoolgirl. Approaching the bars, Karl laid a gentle hand on his shoulder. We burst into tears.

This day, which had begun so well in a shower of light,

in a sunburst of dazzling windowpanes, ended in the deepest gloom.

* * *

Need I relate that our first impulse on returning home was to devise a means of spiriting Karl away from the horrible fate the mayor and his acolytes had decreed for him?

Basically, it was a question of money. My host reviewed his resources; discreetly, I averted my gaze.

But how could I fail to notice that every time he finished his calculations he angrily scratched out his columns and began afresh, hoping no doubt that a new attempt would yield more favorable results? I silently prayed that this would be the case. Alas, each new calculation added to his discouragement.

"No," he muttered at last in defeated tones, "it won't do. It just won't do!"

I had already prepared myself in secret for just such an eventuality. Without a word I reached across the table and handed him the envelope containing six months' salary paid in my name by Morchiev, Morchiev & Sons. (In fact, he himself, armed with my signed endorsement, had gone to collect this sum at the company offices, stubbornly refusing my offer of part of it to cover the cost of my upkeep. "Friendship," he had said with a scowl, "friendship cannot be paid for!" I had lowered my head, covered in shame, even greater shame than I had felt at guzzling his food for nothing.)

He raised his eyes to mine. But his look was so far away that it was quite possible he had failed to recognize the envelope.

"What is this?" he asked.

It was an accusation rather than a question. He was not looking at the envelope but through it. A severe expression crossed his face, drawing his features into rigid lines. I had to screw my courage up to pronounce the single syllable: "Here!"

And like an echo he replied, "No!"

I fought the tremor, at once painful and pleasant, assailing my shoulders, my neck, my throat, my jaws.

"Friendship," I said, "cannot be discussed."

I did not recognize my own voice. At that moment, a single breath of wind could have reduced me to dust and scattered me about the hushed room.

I believe I would have liked that. I know I would have. Deep within us all a bird plumed in sadness yearns for the open sky.

My host had not lifted his gaze from the envelope, but now he was really seeing it, and it alone, and his face was no longer severe. Merely overcome.

"It's for Karl," I said. "It does not concern you."

"For Karl," he said, closing his hand on the envelope.

But, as it happened, my contribution did nothing to alter the verdict of the figures.

All it did was grant the monkey a temporary reprieve. The same kind of reprieve that old Zbylo Morchiev, a committed liberal, granted those who slaved their lives away for him.

It would have taken the salary of someone like Krokody, at the very least, to wipe out the overheads generated by the red brick monkey house, to cover Karl's food and the cost of the props so integral to his art, as well as the emoluments of the obese neurotic knitter at the entrance gate, not to mention (and here I place myself squarely in the perspective of the mayor and aldermen) the lost business opportunities inherent in the absence of an open-air restaurant where the smell of burning fat and the insolence of waitresses with overheated armpits would infallibly attract noisy crowds trailing children lacking either handkerchiefs or shame . . .

Would we be forced to deliver Karl bound hand and foot to that ignominious monster? My benefactor snapped his pencil in despair, hurling the pieces in all directions and covering his face in his enormous hands as he began to swing back and forth on his seat like someone at a wake. It was at that moment that an idea burst like a thunderclap inside my head.

"I have it, comrade!" I cried.

His hands parted and he stared at me in amazement.

"All is not lost! There is still a way!"

"A way?" he mumbled unbelievingly.

Excitement choked me.

"The house!" I managed to croak. "The house my parents left my sister and me and that is now my property! What else could I do with it? I never set foot there anymore. To be frank, I could not bear to go back there, or even to walk past it. In fact, I wish I had never lived there! If you are willing to put up with me a little longer, my friend, the very best thing we could do, if only to keep the house from falling into disrepair and ruin, would be to sell it and everything inside it." As I spoke, my enthusiasm grew; I was almost ready to sally out despite the late hour and start roping in buyers. "My own bed is a straw pallet, I admit, and we would be lucky to have some rag merchant take it off our hands without demanding payment for his pains, but my sister's bed once belonged to the youngest daughter of a prosperous poultry butcher in Bröcznek. It's made of walnut; the frame is supported on eight large chicken feet carved out of a single log, and the headboard is in the form of a rooster with a duck's head, so skillfully rendered that it seems to be watching over the sleep of the person lying in this masterpiece of primitive carpentry. We'd be fools not to get fifty sovereigns for it, perhaps even more! Then there is my father's collection of pornographic erasers and a whole battery of plate lifters, melting spoons, and trick mustard pots that need only a little tinkering to put them back in working order. Then there are the nine silver sugar tongs my grandmother received in full settlement on her wedding day and that my mother barely managed to rescue from the avarice of her sisters. And (don't laugh) there's the mirrored wardrobe in front of which, at the age of fifteen, I spent hours practicing the art of sweeping women off their feet— although I invariably looked like someone carrying a basin of boiling water, and, when I worked on the art of kissing, it looked as if I were whistling a dog to heel, with a Ping-Pong ball in each cheek . . . Nevertheless, that wardrobe would fetch a fortune at one of the antique shops on Dry Tree Street, if only because of its molding and its one-and-a-half-inch-deep false bottom where my mother used to hide her lovers (or so my father joked). Now, what else is there? Why, it would take me all night to draw up a complete inventory . . . "

My friend dissuaded me from going to such trouble, pointing out that I shouldn't be trying to impress him but rather the auctioneer we would hire to handle the sale, so that the latter would do his utmost to drum up customers. My offer could not have been accepted more tactfully and more naturally. Even today, despite what was about to transpire, I cannot remember it without happiness.

Noting my reluctance to return to the haunts of my youth, my friend was determined to take care of everything himself. It was his mistake—just as it was my mistake not to try to dissuade him.

Waking earlier than usual and in great excitement next day, he gulped down his coffee and hurried off to my former residence. I noted mechanically, without attaching particular significance to it, that he had not even asked me the address.

When he returned shortly after noon, more excited than ever (and I must confess that I was scarcely calmer), everything had been arranged.

How had he gone about it? I remember nothing much of his breathless account, interspersed with shouts of laughter and wild cries. But the gist was that he planned to go back as soon as he had lunched (although he was, of course, incapable of swallowing a morsel) in order to supervise the labors of the two movers he had engaged in the market and who were to meet him there at two o'clock.

Postponing until a more propitious moment our celebration of victory, we shared the finger of kümmel remaining in the bottom of a bottle. I recall that, as soon as I saw him cross the threshold, waving his cap as enthusiastically as if he were preparing to cross the seven seas, I had a premonition of doom. But if you were to drop everything because of that sort of feeling—which is most often quite without foundation—life would be purely and simply impossible.

The janitor at number 22 told me all about it (even though he had no liking for me, or perhaps because of that). He was just stepping out into the street when it happened, and the accounts of passersby had allowed him to piece together the chain of events that had provoked it. It would be much too painful for me to give a detailed account here; I beg the reader to excuse me for going straight to the heart of events.

It soon became clear that the mirrored wardrobe would never fit in the stairwell, whose steepness and narrowness, as far back as my memory goes, had always irritated my mother (and inspired certain highly incongruous quips, on which I would prefer to remain silent, from my father). They decided to lower it from my bedroom window, which was on the second floor and looked directly onto the street.

My benefactor, whose grasp of the art of furniture moving was rudimentary, offered to stand in the street and take the weight of the wardrobe as it descended. But, as soon as he saw that huge mass swinging above his head, he realized that he was physically unequal to such a herculean task. The very best he could do was reach up to touch with the tips of his fingers the upper edge of the wardrobe, which was tilting threateningly toward him.

"Stop! Stop!" he cried. "I can't manage it!"

"Everything all right down there?" was the only reply from the mover, who was holding the wardrobe as best he could by its feet.

Make no mistake: The man did not suffer from defective hearing; he had merely, in obedience to the ancestral laws of his guild, sunk that morning's emoluments in drink.

"No!" screamed my friend. "It won't work! Stop! Stop!"

"All right," said the mover. "What shall we do?" His tone clearly implied that he would gladly bend to all his client's whims but that, deep inside, he reserved the right to disapprove of such fantasies.

"You'll have to come down and help," cried my friend. "I can't handle it alone."

"Fine!" the man replied. "When?"

"As quickly as you can!"

"Coming," the man answered absentmindedly, raising his eyes heavenward at this new demonstration of the inconsistency of the leisured classes.

Reaching the door of my bedroom, he was the first to be astounded by the din caused by the mirrored wardrobe's impact with the sidewalk, immediately preceded by the splintering of my companion's skull.

How often since then have I pondered the irony of the coincidence: It was the object that had so often reflected my own image with a fleeting, fumbling voluptuousness that destroyed the man who had revealed me to myself, the man I had approached because I believed we resembled one another. I sensed some lofty philosophical lesson behind all this, but I was and I remain too slow-witted to be able to say what it was.

On a piece of the broken mirror that I picked up mechanically, my hand seemingly guided by a will superior to any human impulse, I recognized with mingled horror and affection the imprint of my friend's face. It was here without the shadow of a doubt that the wardrobe had struck him, his head tilted backward as if to receive Holy Communion, his eyes staring with pathetic disbelief as his likeness fell ever nearer on its way to dashing out his brains.

When I speak of an imprint, I am not being strictly accurate. Naturally the surface of the glass had not been in any way scratched or indented. Nevertheless, every hair of his eyebrows and mustache stood out on the mirror as clearly as if it had been imprinted there.

In fact, this miraculous image called to mind nothing so much as a photographic negative. The nose — because it was on the nose that the weight of the object has first fallen — was no more than a formless smudge, but you could see quite clearly the lines of the forehead and the roots of the hair, the major wrinkles, most of the cheekbones, the aggressive jut of the jaw, and the faintest hairline cracks in both lips; regrettably, though, the absence of eyes gave to the whole the look of a death's-head — or rather, I mean a skeleton's skull.

I slipped this relic furtively under my coat and took it to our home, to that haven with its tinted windows that had borne witness to a fleeting and supreme happiness. In any case, I could not have stood another moment of sympathy — at best hypocritical, at worst frankly derisive — from my former neighbors.

When further disasters followed on the heels of this terrible accident, that simple piece of glass was one of the few souvenirs of that period I was able to keep — the only object to remind me through my worst moments of bitterness and despair that on this earth where I had known such suffering, such evil, such disappointment, I nevertheless had not walked in vain.

There was only one other mourner at my friend's funeral, an old woman, small, skinny, inconsolable, incongruously burdened with a basket from which a leek protruded.

She had taken a seat at the back of the cemetery chapel, so that in order to observe her during the service I was forced to keep looking over my shoulder.

However stupid it may sound, this woman's grief was a great comfort to me, and I was impatient for the ceremony—it was extremely dull—to come to an end so that I could greet her, thank her for attending, and speak with her of the man who had left us (a possibility so far denied me, to my gnawing regret).

Already I was formulating plans to invite her to share the traditional funeral repast with me at Bhirozch's or at Thirsty Whighy's, two modestly priced but respectable establishments where I was almost certain the maître d'hôtel would not show us the door with an imperious forefinger after a glance at my companion's attire, at the enormous holes in her stockings, and at the exhausted leek in her pitiful bag.

But my fellow mourner disappeared as if by magic during the collection; noticing my perplexity, the funeral director explained that the infamous crone had made a perverse practice of attending the funerals of strangers for the past ten years. She had taken up residence in a half-ruined shack near the cemetery gate and attended burials from morning till the chilliest winter nightfalls, wailing out her unrestrained lamentations without having the smallest right to do so.

This was the last straw. I left before the actual interment, realizing with shocking clarity that if I stayed I would be unable to restrain myself from leaping after the coffin into the grave.

Without thinking, I directed my steps toward the Kristophory quarter. I did not know whether my dear departed had been the owner or merely the tenant of his

apartment. I did not know if he had a family somewhere. In fact, I did not even know his name. I had
called him the familiar "you," and that had been quite
enough for us. But since I had not the heart to return to
my parents' house (particularly after what had just happened there), I decided I would go on living in my
friend's home until someone came and threw me out.

I did what I had never done during his long absences:
I went methodically through all his drawers and pockets
and then, finding nothing, through every piece of furniture, every closet, every nook and cranny of the apartment. Still without success.

All I found was a small and very faded sepia photo-
graph of an unknown woman with a towering bun on
whose summit teetered a hat decorated in a fashion that
unmistakably recalled the prize cauliflower exhibit in an
agricultural show; beside her stood a small boy much too
big for his suit and squinting because the sun was in his
face (he had even lifted his right arm to shield his eyes)—
a little boy, in short, who could have been my friend just
as easily as he could have been the Pope or the king of
Prussia. I set this picture on the kitchen sideboard and
wept copiously over it, just in case.

The funeral expenses, the collection, the honoraria, tips, and sundries to the movers (who insisted on receiving hazardous duty pay, pointing out that the wardrobe could just as easily have fallen on their own faces), the padded bill from the entrepreneur who (without my requesting it) had taken it upon himself to clear the public thoroughfare of the debris — all this consumed two-thirds of the sum we had amassed to save Karl.

I had naturally given up the plan that had had such tragic consequences for my friend. And I had to confront the question of household expenses, even though the household consisted of nobody but myself.

I would not last very long on what remained of our nest egg. But it was the very beginning of the month of March, and I would have to wait more than three weeks before I could draw my next pay from the firm of Morchiev, Morchiev & Sons.

In short, if I could prolong the monkey's life for one miserable day without compromising my own vital

needs, it would be the very best that I could hope
to do.

The bleakness of this realization left me without tears,
without any kind of reaction. I merely hoped that the
ground would open up and swallow me, or that someone
(my friend, perhaps?) would slap me on the back and
cheerfully shout, "Wake up! It was just a bad dream!"

But I knew that neither of these things would happen.
I sat there quite still, my eyes staring unseeing into
empty air, and tried to turn myself into stone – not by
willpower but, on the contrary, by the annihilation of
every faculty I possessed. What could happen to a stone?

I was in the little room with the sofa: It was here that I
had first opened my eyes on the setting in which I was to
live so many exhilarating hours, followed by such cruelly
unhappy ones. As evening drew near, everything in the
room (myself included, no doubt) was covered with a
fine, slightly dusty golden film; then darkness slowly
took possession of the room. I had not moved. Nothing,
not even an eyelash. I sensed that night was falling, but I
did not think it. No idea on the subject was born inside
my head. The word "night" did not even flit across my
brain. I did not move. I did not move at all. Not even my
thoughts moved. My thoughts were fixed on one idea:
"Stone – you are stone." Only that. Over and over. With
no other meaning. Light filtered in, and still I did not
move. "You are stone," I thought. The light ebbed away,
and still nothing had moved, either on the surface or
within. Light and dark succeeded one another, nights
and days, and there was no movement. "You are stone,"
and I was stone; I would have become stone, yes, I know I
would have managed it, had the doorbell not rung – and
"ring" is much too weak a word for the barbaric, strident

sound that shattered the slow, numb process of my petrification.

I said earlier that I was registering feelings in a wholly inert fashion, without the slightest mobilization of cerebral processes. I stand by my words. But can one categorize as a "feeling" (with all that the word connotes of lightness, elusiveness, discretion) a racket so ear-shattering and sudden and unexpected that it tumbled me off my chair and drew from me — stone or no stone — a long-drawn-out yell of surprise, if not of terror?

With death in my heart, and determined to put an end to the hideous frenzy of that jangling bell, I pulled my panting frame together. With a pronounced wobble, due to muscle stiffness induced by prolonged immobility, due to lack of food and sleep, due to the paralysis or, at least, the standstill of my mental activity — as well as to the sharp impact of my body against the hard floor — I went to open the door.

And there, once again, I doubted I would be able to hold onto my senses. Side by side and hand in hand on the doormat, canes swinging, straw hats tipped jauntily over one eye, stood Karl and the director of the Kirchenstahl Gardens. While the director pressed with all his weight on the doorbell, as if he had sworn to push the button deep into the door frame, Karl, in perfect symmetry, was pushing his own finger against exactly the same spot on the other side of the frame.

I was incapable of the smallest sound. I was vaguely aware that my lower jaw had dropped to my chest the way saliva trails down from a baby's mouth, but I could not have stared at them with greater astonishment if they had been the devil and his wife.

Yet no other callers on earth could have brought me greater comfort, if not exactly pleasure. These two beings had at least known my friend. They had been granted the good fortune to appreciate the extent of his gifts, his soaring intelligence, his good and essentially sunny spirit, his altruism, his extraordinary skills as a connoisseur both of monkeys and, if I may say so, of men, his astonishingly precise vocabulary, his modesty, his limitless culture (ranging from the minutiae of local architectural history through the subtleties of arithmetic to the art of eating shellfish), the perfection of his tastes, and his habit of wrinkling his nose when he encountered an unpleasant smell.

On top of all that, we all three knew the esteem in which he had held the director (even leaping to take the latter's part in a squalid mayoral intrigue), the friendship he had so freely bestowed on me, and the unflagging affection (to understate the case) he had lavished on the monkey Karl, whose talents, professional conscience, and some even rarer quality (a quality so elusive no word can do it justice) had first satisfied his demanding mind and then found a way to his heart.

Yes, all that united us was the sad and gentle memory of the deceased. But that common memory was stronger than a bronze chain.

"May we come in, Mister Ghichka?" inquired the director with a politeness rarely encountered these days. "Would your friend be so good as to admit us?"

Alas, alas, for the third time I swooned . . .

When I had returned to my senses and delivered the terrible news, the director, scratching me gently behind the ear in an effort to soothe my pain, declared in melancholy tones, "Just imagine, brave Mister Ghichka:

But a short while ago the municipal council met in extraordinary session at the behest of the mayor and his clique with the sole aim of pronouncing Karl's death sentence. Happily, I was forewarned by a councilman whom I had once been fortunate enough to extract from an ugly bribery scandal, thanks to a false witness." (I tried hard not to look at the monkey, who was firing an imaginary rifle in all directions from the foot of the sofa.) "I did not hesitate. I opened the cage. Karl and I leapt onto my motorcycle and we raced here without losing a second. Drawing courage from our conversation last Sunday, I had hoped that your friend would consent to take Karl in. Alas, I could not have foreseen . . . "

He collapsed.

Raising him gently, I drew him close, rocked him in my arms, and tried desperately to scratch his head in my turn; but his despair was too great (or perhaps I simply lacked the skill).

Need I add that, when he left me, looking twenty years older but nonetheless at peace with himself, I had consented to take Karl under my wing and to cherish him as if my own blood flowed in his veins?

It was not even necessary for me to show the monkey around the apartment. You could have sworn he had lived there all his life.

Scarcely had the director taken his leave than my new companion marched straight to the hall and hung up his straw hat and cane. Then he headed without a moment's hesitation for the deceased's bedroom, opened the closet, slipped on the rather threadbare robe my friend had been so fond of, selected a mauve handkerchief from the appropriate drawer, folded it with casual elegance and — with a heartbreakingly familiar gesture — tucked it into his breast pocket.

He then rejoined me in the living room and switched on the wireless, giving the right-hand side of the apparatus the small sharp tap without which it would never function.

I must confess that at this juncture the monkey's antics struck me as almost sacrilegious. In fact, I was on the verge of putting an end to them when the following occurred to me: Since I was not going to find any peace in remembrance, I had no reason to cut short behavior that (on reflection) owed much more to invocation than to evocation; seen from this perspective, the monkey's conduct demonstrated at least as much fervor and piety as my own vain jeremiads.

The director of the Kirchenstahl Gardens had pressed on me a tidy sum of money, representing a whole quarter's tips and emoluments originally earmarked for the inept ticket-office woman; he himself intended to flee on the motorcycle to the frontier, crossing it at night between Ghlo and Ghno, a region of hardy forests where the frontier guards are reputed to be congenital half-wits; then to cross featureless Podolia in the direction of Odessa, there to seek hire as a top-mizzen man, or a bellringer, or a part-time coal trimmer on some merchant vessel — if possible a banana boat, for reasons easily guessed at — and then, anchors aweigh for Maracaibo! In any case, the animal and I would be safe from want for a while.

I never again heard from this extraordinary person who, out of loyalty to the anthropoid, to himself, and to his dream of a civilized world, had cut himself off forever from the company of the animal, had without a second thought abandoned his wife, children, garden, job, country, and reputation, and had exposed his naked breast to the vengeful blade of justice. But every time I mentioned him (or simply conjured up his features in my head), Karl would turn down the radio, leave my friend's armchair and bathrobe, bring the cane and straw hat in from the hall, and give a bravura rendering of his hero that (had the latter been able to witness it) would have rewarded him a hundredfold for his sacrifice.

He particularly liked to pose with left leg forward, right leg bent slightly back, and, with his face lifted to the ocean breezes, to survey vast horizons with an air of wounded dignity and fierce determination. Then, himself again, he bowed low, sweeping the floor with his hat in salute to the sublime allegory he had just created.

The knitting ticket taker also came in for her share. He cut old newspapers into small rectangles, stuffed them in an enamel basin, and frantically raised and lowered his rear end into it with an air of imbecilic, vacuous greed.

Then it was the mayor's turn. I had never laid eyes on him, but I instantly recognized the shifty eyes, the fat Austrian cigars, the potbelly straining beneath a waistcoat bound by a double watch chain, and his trick of talking out of the corner of his mouth as if he were spitting out nutshells.

Then there were the movers, the janitor at number 22, the old fraud from the cemetery, the funeral director and the priest, Krokody, Zbylo Morchiev, Maria Wakhelyana, my sister, my father, my mother, my grandmother with her regiment of sugar tongs, Aunt Filimor, the doctor who had so judiciously commented on the precariousness of human life, the schoolmaster, the dairy-truck driver, his truck, his milk cans, his flawless instincts, and much more. Everything was fair game. All our parties really needed was a little sparkling wine.

My God! I certainly was in no mood for jesting, but I laughed and laughed until I thought I could never stop. It was as if laughing had taken the place of breathing for me.

Yes, that laughter was the breath of life regaining possession of my beleaguered body, so recently almost overcome by the apnea of death. And I owed it to all who were dead, as well as to my own dear dead one, not to stand in the way of that breath of life — for to each his own, whatever the price: Death for the dead and life for the living.

By the grace of this divinely inspired primate, I was reliving the intense joy and the intense surge of love my friend had felt outside his cage that autumn morning in that recent and remote time when I had not even known who I was. And, by reliving all this, I was drinking at the wellsprings of life itself.

Almost every evening now, rather than listen to the generally mediocre dramas on the wireless, or to the news bulletins that seemed to peddle an even more mediocre caricature of those same dramas (but I understood nothing of these noises from the outside world and took not the slightest interest in them), I ensconced myself in an easy chair while Karl, his genius daily more dazzling, breathed life into the portrait gallery I have just described.

Sometimes his art scaled such heights that I had to strain to convince myself that I was looking at a reproduction and not the original.

One evening, in fact, his mimicry was so compelling that I leapt from my chair and hugged him to my bosom, believing I was embracing my own sister.

Nor was this an isolated experience. Another time, it was only after I had shaved carefully in front of the mirror that I realized there was no mirror, but that I was nose to nose with the mischievous simian. He had utterly misled me throughout the operation!

The fact is, we were as happy together as it is possible for two creatures to be when happiness is no longer permitted them. Submerged though we were in fathomless distress, we nevertheless inhaled the perfumes of our lost paradise. Which conclusively proves that art—even when it is simply the art of striking poses and making faces—unleashes forces far surpassing those natural to the human being (and, needless to say, to the animal as well).

The twenty-fifth was a Wednesday. How could I ever forget it? The doorbell rang. We gasped and stared at each other. I know that the monkey and I were thinking the same thing: "Could this be the director back again?"

Yet our instincts told us no. But if not, then who? It was incomprehensible to me how people managed to find our address. Karl and his master, for instance: What had guided their steps here, given that they had no clearer idea than I of my friend's identity (always assuming his name and address were to be found in some directory)?

I supposed that our caller was some distant relative of my unhappy companion. He would have heard by chance of the death, and now here he was, elevated by circumstance to the status of outright heir of a vague uncle or cousin one hundred times removed—and flanked by a bailiff and perhaps by policemen — to claim his inheritance and toss us into the street.

If I was right, Karl would be seized and carted off to the city pound within the hour.

The reader will appreciate the new depths of sorrow and anguish into which I sank. Like a condemned man walking to the scaffold, I covered the distance to the front door. Trembling from head to foot, ready to swoon all over again, I put my hand on the knob. Like a robot, like a sleepwalker in a nightmare, I closed my hand on it. I turned it. I pulled the door open.

It was Maria Wakhelyana.

"**G**ood heavens!" she said, wrinkling her lovely lip in disdain. "It's poor Ghichka!"

Poor indeed, and so dumfounded he dares not attempt to describe it!

"Is your master at home?" inquired this paragon of feminine grace.

"My master?" I stammered.

Had she suddenly gone mad? Or was it I who had lost my reason as a result of all these disasters and monkey tricks? My perplexity brought helpless tears to my eyes.

"As sharp as ever!" said Maria Wakhelyana sarcastically. "Come on, Ghichka, my man, I have no intention of standing on these stairs forever. They stink of cabbage soup!"

I realized that in my terror I had neglected to greet her.

"Good morning, Miss Maria Wakhelyana," I burst out in a voice that fear, emotion, and wonder had turned into that of a braying ass.

The young lady's eyes narrowed to blazing slits.

"Are you being impertinent?" she hissed between clenched teeth (and what teeth, dear God! they were like pearls!). "I have the feeling you're not going to last very long in your new job."

Then she opened her mouth wide, leaned forward, and shrieked into my face, "Announce me to Mister Folykhulo this minute, you fool!"

Half-sobbing, I replied, "But . . . there is no Mister Folykhulo here, Miss Maria Wakhelyana."

Hands on hips, she eyed me like a snake, ready to accuse me of lying. But no doubt it crossed her mind that a young man like me would never have dared to behave so insolently toward her; there must have been at least some truth in my words.

"How so?" she asked warily, still eyeing me with suspicion.

"Well," I began, deeply embarrassed, "I am the one who lives in this apartment, Miss Maria Wakhelyana . . . " (I burned to kiss her feet; failing that, the hem of her dress.)

"Oh!" she suddenly gasped, giving a graceful little birdlike hop on the doormat.

I followed her gaze.

"That is the monkey," I said. "Please be so kind as to come in."

To my great surprise, she accepted.

"Now, Ghichka," she said to me, her tones somewhat softer. "This is 33A, is it not?"

"The very same," I said foolishly.

"Second floor overlooking the street?"

"Exactly, Miss Maria Wakhelyana."

By now she was almost as perplexed as I was.

"And you do not know a Mister Folykhulo?"

"No."

She thought for a moment, her gaze far away. Behind her I could see that Karl was already studying her with the obvious intention of adding another portrait to our gallery.

"Well . . . that is," I continued, "someone else did live here once."

She grabbed my arm.

"Wasn't his name Folykhulo? It's not exactly an everyday name. Try to remember. Rack your brains. Think!"

I gave her a sheepish smile.

"I would love to, Miss Maria Wakhelyana, I would be so happy to do that for you. But, you see, the trouble is I never knew what this man's name was, and yet we lived here together for more than six months."

"Then it can't be him," she said at once. (Karl had already mastered her frown, the palpitation of her nostrils, and that faint — that imperceptible — squint that made her even more desirable.)

As we talked, we crossed the hall and entered the living room.

"Won't you sit down for a while?" I asked. "I'll make tea. There's no more sparkling wine, I'm afraid."

Her gaze was absent again.

"Wait," she said. "What did he look like?"

"Uh . . . he looked a little bit like me," I said.

"Lord!" she said.

(Crouched beneath the sideboard, Karl was meticulously studying her wonderful little feet.)

I had a sudden inspiration. "I have a photo!" I shouted in triumph.

With one leap I was in the kitchen; I snatched the picture from the cupboard and returned to place it in her hands. (The monkey was lifting the hem of her skirt with a puzzled look.)

Maria Wakhelyana took one look at the photo, then it slipped from her fingers. "It is he!" she breathed. "There can be no doubt. Benazar Folykhulo! Merciful heaven!"

Karl picked up the photo and began to examine it from all angles.

"Would you like a liqueur, Miss Maria Wakhelyana?" I asked, worried at the violent effect the document had had on her frail constitution.

She shook her head.

"That's good," I said. "We don't have any."

I truly believe that I had lost my sense of time and space. And, as if to add to my woes, the monkey was looking back and forth from the photo to our visitor's face, leading me to suspect that he was speculating about a possible relationship between Miss Maria Wakhelyana and the woman with the cauliflower hat.

Making tea gave me an excellent excuse to escape and collect my wits alone in the kitchen; but suddenly I remembered that there was no tea at all in the house: Karl hated it. So had my friend—this man who, it seemed, had gone under the excessively odd name of Ebenezer . . . well, something like that.

While all these thoughts were chasing one another through my head, forming an ever more tangled skein, the young lady (whose strength of character I had always admired) was once more wholly mistress of herself; she was rather impatiently watching Karl, who kept raising two fingers to his forehead to signify that he was at her service for one of his imitations.

"Karl would like to give you an imitation of one of the human species we've come across," I said hastily. "He's very good at it, aren't you, Karl? What would you like? The old woman who tends the geese? The flamenco dancer? The accounting clerk?"

"Couldn't he imitate a monkey leaving the room?" inquired Miss Maria Wakhelyana, with a flash of that caustic humor that was merely one of the thousand jeweled facets of her personality.

"He would imitate the room itself if you so wished, dear Miss Wakhelyana," I murmured urbanely. (But, to be frank, I have never been a wit, and my lame sally met with the glacial reception it deserved.)

"Tell me, Ghichka," the young lady went on in somewhat tentative tones, as if her thoughts were pulling her words along. "Did you really know this man?"

"I owe him everything!" I declared proudly. "The most extraordinary being I have ever encountered, and we were as close as two fingers on the same hand."

The monkey wagged two fingers seemingly welded together by some superhuman force beneath Maria Wakhelyana's nose, but she barely glanced at him.

"Were you his servant?" she asked.

I placed my palm on my sweater at the spot where I believed my heart to be beating.

"On my honor, on my life, Miss Maria Wakhelyana, I proclaim in absolute truth that it was this incomparable being, this Balthazar or whatever, who made himself my servant—mine, a poor devil unfit to lick the soles of his shoes!"

Abruptly she jerked her feet back under the chair to avoid Karl's greedy lips.

"He must have been in some kind of trouble," she mused with a frown. "A gambling debt, no doubt . . . "

"He never gambled!" I proclaimed ringingly. (I knew that, in that instant, I rivaled the greatest tragedians of my day.) "He had no vices!"

Rapidly the monkey sketched a parody of the most degrading vices with one hand, while making furious gestures of repudiation with the other. Without paying him the slightest attention, Maria Wakhelyana smiled a knowing smile to herself. I was deeply moved by it, but it vanished quickly.

"All right!" she said. "What has become of him?"

The roots of my hair tingled. Karl closed sorrowful eyes and banged his temples with his fists.

"Become of him?" I whimpered. "Nothing has become of him, Miss Maria Wakhelyana. He died three weeks ago."

She jumped to her feet as if on a spring.

"Died? Did you kill him?"

All I could do was gasp for breath, flap my hands frantically before my face, and roll horrified eyes. At my feet, Karl was playing dead. In my confusion, the idea drove like a dagger into my heart—that I was indeed responsible for the death of Zazana . . . whatever.

Had it not been for me, he would never have encountered that fatal wardrobe. I had forced his destiny. I had not even sought to detain him—him, my only friend—after heaven in its infinite mercy had sent me a premonition of the disaster about to occur . . .

Yes, Miss Maria Wakhelyana, yes, Karl, my excellent monkey, this so-called accident was nothing less than murder; and the guilty one, the prime mover in this abomination, now stood before you!

61

"How can it be?" the young lady wailed. "He who was such a lover of life! He who was so . . . handsome is not the word . . . " She groped for a more appropriate term, but sorrow had briefly dulled the edge of her incisive mind. She gave up. "He who was so generous."

"Was he not? Was he not?" I wept.

But it was pointless. The little bird did not even hear me, so deep was her despair.

"He said such sweet things to me," she went on. "He called me his sugar dove and his little blue bunny! For love of me he stripped whole gardens of roses and begonias! He took me to the fairground! He bought me triple-scoop ice creams! He covered his arms to the elbows with cooking fat just for the pleasure of holding my little bag of fries! He knew my beauty spots by heart! He kissed me passionately on the mouth whenever I sang for him!"

"How about that?" I gulped.

"He nibbled my earlobe at the theater! He went into ecstasies when I swallowed oysters! He let me keep the change when we went shopping! Is it possible that I must now say good-bye to all that?" (With an air of fathomless grief, the monkey waved farewell to a silhouette vanishing behind the wireless set.) "Mother Mary! My Benazar! Dead! Dead! He who was so mischievous! So cultivated! Tell me it is not so! What happened? What became of him? Ghichka, I implore you, do not leave me in this terrible uncertainty, tell me all! Tell me he did not suffer!"

"He was in the street," I said, the light of insanity already kindling in the depths of my gaze. "It was fated that he be hit on the head by a mirrored wardrobe."

"God in heaven!" she replied. "Just like my three brothers!"

Mechanically, I stretched out my arms, expecting her to swoon into them. Instead, she displayed a steadfastness that increased my admiration for her, if that was possible, tenfold.

"And now," she said, firm as a rock, "who will pay my rent?"

Karl, his face a pitiless, uncaring mask, pretended to be collecting rents in a tenement building while ignoring the pleas of a desperate young woman.

Maria Wakhelyana suddenly sat down again and began to drum her fingers on her knees (through her dress, of course).

"He could have warned me, the swine!" she gritted.

This high-spirited reaction, at such a time, fired my enthusiasm all over again, and I gazed at her with renewed adoration. She did not notice, however, for she had begun a detailed inspection of the furnishings and decoration of the house. It was almost as if she were drawing up a mental inventory.

"And who inherits all this?" she finally asked.

I opened my mouth and simultaneously realized that I did not know the answer. At that moment Karl drew near and, presumably in order to convey his sympathy, laid his hand on my shoulder.

"You, Ghichka?" asked Maria Wakhelyana, misunderstanding the gesture. "You are his heir?"

I should have denied it. I should have protested to the skies that it was not so. But she had cooed those words so musically, so caressingly (particularly my name), so voluptuously, that I did not have the heart. For fear that she would never speak to me like that again.

It was pure weakness on my part, I admit, but I have never claimed to be spartan. (And, besides, if I tried to hide a fox inside my shirt, the first policeman I came across would drag me off by the ear to answer charges of poaching.) I was quite simply unable to cause Miss Maria Wakhelyana the slightest pain. Had she called me a coach driver, a blockhead, a Pekingese, I would have acquiesced. All things considered, being designated a great man's heir seemed infinitely preferable.

No excuse can efface or even mitigate the crime of usurping another man's identity, for God has conceived us to be what we are and not what he has charged our neighbor with being. Nevertheless, I would point out that, while I made no move to disabuse the young woman, nor did I attempt to encourage her in her error.

All I really did was allow her to interpret Karl's gesture as she saw fit; after all, it was ordinary enough to mean any number of things, or nothing at all. Many times in my life I have seen people lay a hand on someone else's shoulder without signifying that the person in question had inherited anything at all! But the truth is that, if I had not been madly in love with Maria Wakhelyana at that time, I would not be trying to advance such flagrantly dishonest arguments.

But I *was* in love. That is, I was burning to draw her into some quiet corner—and prostrate myself at her feet.

Should I say more in celebration of the delicate beauty of her features, the freshness of her complexion, her bewitching roguishness, her sparkling wit? It would be useless. Would I have fallen into ecstasies before her if she had not combined in the very highest degree every attraction of which a woman may rightfully boast?

And, even long ago, when I had rebelled against the contempt with which she had withered my shy attempts to woo her, and, even when I had laughed myself silly over the not-so-attractive picture the monkey had created of her (before he had met her, that is, and was forced to rely on the model painted for him by my vengeful spirit — which he read like an open book), even then I had not ceased loving her.

Proud as I was, I might have tried to persuade myself of the contrary, but I loved her passionately and had done so from the first second I saw her. I could not even conceive that a single man on earth could waste his time dreaming of any other woman.

And so, on learning that my departed companion had worshiped her with a fervor at least comparable to my own, I was, so to speak, quite unsurprised. It seemed to me to belong perfectly to the order of things.

And let me say right away that I felt no jealousy either. If he had still been of this world, I swear I would have condemned my own feelings to silence (in any case, they were not requited — how could they have been?) and instead looked with favor on their rendezvous, encouraged their bliss, borne their love letters from one end of town to the other; in short, I would have intrigued in every way imaginable to promote the happiness that was theirs by reason of their staggering superiority to the rest of the human race.

The reader may doubt me if he wishes, but I declare that their happiness in one another was amply sufficient for my own happiness. And I felt honored, to say the least, that a man like Benar . . . Bazar — I just can't get that name into my head — that such an exceptional man should have chosen as the object of his undying love the same young woman as a person as ordinary as myself. I marveled at it and found in it a reason not to despair utterly over my shortcomings.

So, when my friend had left the house after breakfast, generally to remain away until the afternoon was drawing to an end, it was with no other purpose than to visit Miss Maria Wakhelyana and spend unforgettable moments in her company. Merciful God! Why had he not left earlier? Why had he not let me languish there for longer periods? In his place . . . but I must not blaspheme.

I had imagined him busy with obscure duties, such as delivering pithy addresses from the platforms of street-cars — and all the time he had been nibbling the adorable girl's earlobes! Without turning a hair, he had been paying the rent on her little nest! With a smile on his lips and a hand in his wallet. A man whose likes we shall not see again.

That was why the problem of the monkey's upkeep had thrown his budget into such upheaval: He had to subsidize Miss Maria Wakhelyana's upkeep as well — and mine, too, since he had refused all my offers to help shoulder costs! Yes, that man would have given the shirt off his back — if need be, to a wholesale shirt dealer — rather than risk failing in his Christian duties.

That day, Wednesday, March 25, Maria Wakhelyana was extremely kind to me. She deigned to laugh heartily at jokes that were not always in the best of taste and, in any case, never very funny. She clapped wildly at the (admittedly brief) glimpse Karl gave her — at *her* request, I might add — of his talents.

He did half the one-legged man, a small segment of the man serving a life sentence (which, to be candid, did not amount to much), the merest hint of the cherry picker, and finished with a bizarrely composite sequence in which I identified fragments of a packer, of a Parisian, of a road-accident victim, of a trombonist, and of a Madonna of the sleeping cars. Whatever he did, the young lady made no effort to mask her rapture. Her laughter left her breathless, and, whenever she was forced to avert her gaze from the spectacle for fear of losing her breath completely, she plied me with questions about the inheritance that had fallen to me (and that could not have fallen to a more deserving person, as she kept repeating).

With that care for precision that marks the practical woman, the kind woman who keeps an impeccable home for her husband, she lingered over details a less sensible person might have dismissed as trivial: the surface area and orientation of the apartment, the state of the silverware, the date of purchase of the radio, and so forth.

We parted very good friends, I believe. From her point of view, I mean; as for me, I had long since gone hopelessly beyond the friendship stage . . .

I dreamed of her all night long. In one of my dreams she removed her overskirt in order to play quoits with me, and I clearly glimpsed the swelling curve of her calf. The reader may gauge my perturbation when she appeared very early next morning bearing a half-dozen hot croissants wrapped in tissue paper.

And the same every morning after that.

Maria Wakhelyana said that we had to support and solace one another in our common bereavement. And we did support one another, with the greatest energy. In fact, I do not believe it possible to give more mutual support without overstepping the bounds of decency.

Toward eleven o'clock she would take over the kitchen, in order, as she put it, to "cook up a little something." Karl liked to hide in the corridor and spring out on me whenever I passed by to give me the impression that Maria Wakhelyana had come from the living room, although I had just left her in the pantry! After a month I was no longer fooled, but I went on exclaiming, "Oh, Miss Maria Wakhelyana!" whenever he did it so as not to spoil his fun. For he, too, needed support and solace.

Evening would fall and still the young miss would not take her leave. I shall not go so far as to say that we had to push her out, but very often it was dark by the time she decided to depart, and I could not help thinking of the disapproving remarks such conduct would inspire in the neighborhood. Just think! A young woman shutting herself in from morning till night with two vigorous bachelors, one of them a monkey . . . It made me shudder. Karl bucked my spirits up a little by miming an allegory of scandal that was a pure masterpiece of wit and social satire.

"Ghichka," Maria Wakhelyana said to me one day in the corridor as I moved to bury my fist in her midriff (for Karl's little joke, repeated ad nauseam, was beginning to get on my nerves), "Ghichka, do you know how wonderful you are?"

She seized my shoulders violently and pressed me to her, shuddering all over as if I were not a tactful and reserved man but a kind of jackhammer. She gripped me more brutally than ever and, to my terror, began to grunt filthy words into my ear.

The wedding took place the next week in the strictest intimacy—that is to say, in the presence of Karl and, as our second witness, the arrogant beggar who hung about the precincts of Saint Barnabas and All Saints (I should mention in passing that the dean took it upon himself to ask several highly indiscreet questions about the latter). The ceremony was followed by a simple but wholesome meal at the Crowned Hart Inn, where, Miss Maria Wakhelyana confided, she had once worked on Sundays and holidays as a part-time waitress.

I had done my utmost to dissuade her from linking her destiny with mine. I knew full well that I was not wonderful and that I was not the possessor (despite her panting allegations) of a big juicy cucumber. Not that I was what people choose to call deficient in that area, but nothing could justify such excessive claims. In short, I was what I was. It was inevitable that I should disappoint her. I had warned her, and the monkey was my witness. She had refused to take heed; in fact, I could scarcely articulate my arguments through her hungry kisses. And what had to happen happened.

We were no sooner joined in the eyes of God and man than Miss Maria Wakhelyana was rudely awakened to my shortcomings, despite all my efforts not to conceal them from her. She began to berate me, to shower me with reproaches (charging me in particular with taking advantage of her innocence and frailty), and to rain blows on me with her parasol.

I deserved all I got. The unhappy child could scarcely find words to convey my idleness, my stupidity, my body odors, my lopsided features, my lewdness. At the very thought that she had been forced to throw away her best years in the company of such a wet blanket, she would hurl herself at me and claw at my eyes.

I understood her. I understood her all too well! I strove — ineffectually — to be the least hateful I could. I yoked myself to kitchen duties, for she had no intention, as she put it, of becoming "the servant of a goat." This at least gave me the satisfaction of knowing that she was not saddled with tasks that were beneath her.

All day long, as I scoured, scrubbed, rubbed, washed, and ironed her lacy wear (with the precious help of the monkey, whose habit of imitating every task meant he was now capable of carrying them all out himself), she struggled with her migraine by stuffing herself with Turkish delight, dolefully stretched out on the sofa in the small room—that piece of furniture she told me I was to call a "divan" when company was present. What company? The point remained a mystery to me.

Exasperated by the wearisome, daily discovery of further defects in my character, she no longer derived pleasure from Karl's pantomimes. On the contrary, the unfortunate simian had only to seize an (imaginary) dentist's pliers or load an (imaginary) stepladder onto his back for her to approach nervous prostration. "That monkey! That monkey!" she would wail. "What have I done to deserve this?" I had to take Karl to one side to beg his forgiveness.

When I went out to the market, I asked him to come with me; as soon as we were outside we would slip into an alleyway, where he was free to offer me a command performance of his latest creations—except for the day someone loosed his dog on us, claiming that our antics were an affront to the divine image in which man is made.

But these were happy moments. The animal's genius blossomed daily. Karl even reached the stage of anticipating his models' behavior. One morning, for example, taking on Miss Maria Wakhelyana's appearance, he made the gesture of emptying something on my head. That very evening she crowned me with the chamber pot because I had murmured to her that she was the most beautiful of women.

One of my spouse's habitual complaints sprang from the fact that I obliged her to live in penury after promising her the lap of luxury.

I soon realized that she suspected me of embezzling, for my own purposes, the fat wad of bills that she had felt in the days when my friend had hugged her to his breast.

However ill-founded this suspicion, how could I defend myself against it? All my protestations seemed merely attempts to hoodwink her. First she made veiled allusions to it, then outright accusations, then she clawed at me and lashed out with the parasol.

Since I was unable to produce this nonexistent nest egg (and since the monkey, stung by her coldness toward him, took malicious pleasure in erecting vertiginous piles of gold pieces whenever she glanced in his direction), she altered her tactics and trained the formidable artillery of her charms on me.

"What a stag you are!" she panted, eyes popping from her head. "What a great foaming stag you are, Ghichka!"

And I almost was: She drove me out of my mind. I certainly foamed. Attempting to emulate me, the monkey was seized with a violent coughing spasm.

But neither that nor the pressing offer of her charms that Miss Maria Wakhelyana made at the drop of a hat, once even pursuing me as far as Weiss's Bakery — nothing summoned up even the smallest bank note in our house. On the other hand, the purchase of a hat with a veil and of an article I dare not mention here dug a hole in our household resources that virtually liquidated the sum we had inherited from the director of the Kirchenstahl Gardens.

When I confessed this to the woman who had given me the best years of her life, she first rent the air with imprecations and then, armed with a kitchen knife, proceeded to disembowel armchairs, cushions, and mattresses, and to chop splinters of wood from the floors. I have no idea why Karl, a funnel perched upside down on his head, chose to play the fool throughout this harrowing scene.

At least this dreadful episode shook me out of my lethargy.

In a flash I remembered that I was not simply an idle heir and an extraordinarily repulsive bridegroom (although quite capable of foaming from time to time) but also an accounting clerk at the house of Morchiev, Morchiev & Sons, to whom that house (in an unheard-of exception to its rules, and only because of the diplomatic intervention of a man regrettably mirrored-wardrobed for the sole crime of leaping to the rescue of a monkey threatened with the firing squad), to whom that house had granted a year's paid leave of absence as well as a wage increase. The upheavals that had preceded, accompanied, and followed my marriage had wiped it from my mind. I had not gone to collect my wages for March, and it was now April 30. Two months' pay awaited me—not much, but better than nothing, particularly in our critical circumstances.

Next morning I borrowed Karl's straw hat, which looked smarter on me than my floppy cap and went out into the driving rain.

"Straw hat coming!" shouted the doorman the instant he set eyes on me, and shot away as if his pants were on fire.

I had to fight my way through the janitors before I was finally admitted into the presence of chief accountant Ghroblo. Barring the way with a wall of chests, they pointed out to me that that model employee was not accustomed to seeing radicals or fops during working hours.

"Let me through! Let me through!" I protested as they pressed in on me from all sides. "Can't you see I'm only Mister Ghichka?"

Not that I cared very much what these flunkies thought. I could not have said whether their faces were familiar or not. All underlings look alike. But my blood froze in my veins when Ghroblo shot me a weary look from the underbrush of his enormous eyebrows and failed to recognize me.

"Ghichka Piktopek," I exclaimed, stretching out a hand.

"He isn't here," he mumbled sullenly.

"I *am* Ghichka Piktopek!" I screamed.

He did not even look up from his eternal paperwork.

"Impossible," he growled. "He no longer works here."

Eyes standing out of my head, mouth hanging open, I gaped at him. So certain did he seem that I was tempted to go to the lavatory and check in the mirror there to see whether I actually was the man I claimed to be.

Admittedly, this Ghroblo had always been the butt of derisive snickers. First of all, he had a ridiculous name. And he was the father of an excessively fat daughter (so fat, said the office wags, that you needed two trips to take her to a dance). But to leap from that to seeing him as a humorist, a deadpan joker, or a vaudeville clown like my father was a step nothing would persuade me to take.

On the contrary, the fellow was a notorious grump. One day, after removing from his left buttock an Amiral No. 5 positioned skillfully on his seat by mischievous associates, he had found nothing better to do than to have it framed and displayed over his desk with the handwritten caption, "Souvenir of a bunch of asses."

Around me the flunkies were flapping their arms.

"Well? Well?" they yapped. "What did we tell you?" I was suddenly helpless and deeply unhappy.

"Mister Ghroblo," I begged, my throat constricted. "Please!"

"Hey, Ghroblo, this popinjay's come to ask for your daughter's hand!" yelled someone behind me.

They were giggling shamelessly. It was odious.

"Ghroblo?" I said again, my voice wretched. "Ghroblo, my friend?"

"Yes? What can I do for you?"

Good God, now he could not even remember me from a few seconds ago! He already thought I was a new visitor. From the very depths of my despair, my stomach in knots, my heart hammering wildly, I bawled through my sobs, "Ghroblo, you old fool! You heap of whale shit! It's me, Ghichka! Ghichka Piktopek! Pik-to-pek! PIKTOPEK!"

I suspect it was the noise that attracted assistant manager Krokody's attention.

"What is going on here?" he asked in his creaking-door voice. "Are you drunk again, Mister Ghroblo?"

The chief accountant started to tremble like an autumn leaf, but the satisfaction this gave me was short-lived, for already the withering gaze of old Zbylo Morchiev's right-hand man was upon me.

Today I have the distinct feeling that I was not a good pleader of my case. I tried to say too much. I was too emotional. What's more, I have never been an articulate speaker, and Mister Krokody had always cast a paralyzing spell on my colorless personality.

I am afraid I jumbled up the box of chocolates and the lilies, Mehury Ghroblo's insolence, the leave of absence granted me because of my condition, the intervention of my deceased friend, my wages for March and April, Miss Maria Wakhelyana's groundless suspicions, her hat and veil, and the boundless generosity of Morchiev, Morchiev & Sons.

"Just slow down," assistant manager Krokody told me. "What is that ridiculous name you keep parroting?"

"Mehury Ghroblo?"

"No, not that. I know him only too well!" He destroyed the chief accountant with a glare. "Another name."

"Banar—"

"No, no, no!"

"Zbyl- -"

"Silence, you insolent swine! Another!"

"Miss Maria Wakhelyana?"

He merely shrugged. I felt myself turn pale.

"You cannot mean . . . Ghich—"

"Yes! Yes! That's the one!"

"—ka Piktopek," I finished on a dying note that might as well have been my swan song.

"Piktopek, yes, yes, that's it," said the assistant manager, eyes half-closed as he nibbled reflectively on a thumbnail. "I seem to remember we had someone here with that name . . . "

"That's right!" I burst out. "In fact—"

He stopped me with an irritated gesture.

"Don't tell me! It'll come back . . . Piktopek . . . Piktopek . . . Oh yes, I remember! Piktopek, Ghichka, disputed-claims department, third bay on the right, near the window. No future, like all the others. A rather self-effacing young man, wasn't he? Perhaps he used his eraser too liberally?" A loud, rasping laugh bent him double. It was the first time I had ever seen him laugh; a second sooner I would not have believed it possible. "Piktopek, my God! Where the devil did he dig that name up? Oh, yes, I remember him well! It's not every day you come across such total imbeciles. Incurable, I'd say. Not a shred of ability; no initiative at all. A straw scarecrow, yes, a scarecrow would have performed better. Piktopek, eh? Ghichka Piktopek? Oh, my, my, yes! Not to mention his unappealing appearance, don't you agree, Mister-Ghroblo-pretend-ing-to-add-up-your-accounts-but-actually-listening-to-every-word-I'm-saying-and-who'll-stay-on-for-an-hour-after-the-others-have-left? Ah, my dear sir" (he had turned back to me), "Piktopek had all the appeal of a mackerel on a slab! If only you could have seen him! How can I do justice to such a clown? No normal person, no matter how much he screwed up his face, could hope to give you an idea of what he looked like! For instance, he . . . "

And here he launched into a description of my person that, in all objectivity, applied more closely to Karl than to me.

It was quite horrible. And that was not all. With hideous gusto, he now began to mimic my posture and gait ("An ostrich egg, my dear sir! He must have been holding an ostrich egg between his buttocks!") and the way I used to greet him, sweeping my cap amid the dirt and debris on the ground (what point was there in pointing out that I had never possessed a cap, or even considered possessing one?).

"Even someone like Mehury Ghroblo," he said in conclusion, "is a less pathetic specimen than Ghichka Piktopek! We threw him out, of course. Mister Kharnivor Morchiev (far too soft-hearted a man, as I often tell him) wanted to take him onto his personal payroll to change the light bulbs and feed the dog—you know the kind of thing I mean—but I felt it my duty to intervene. 'You'll regret it once he's eaten all your light bulbs and stuffed Monsieur Jean's (that's the dog) tail into the electric outlet,' I told him. Mister Kharnivor Morchiev shuddered and, to thank me for my advice, offered me a cigar from the second box (the first being reserved, of course, for the exclusive use of the gentlemen's clients). And so, to the relief of us all, the pitiful Mister Piktopek was asked to remove himself. Don't tell me you've run across him?"

I told him nothing. Nothing at all. I bade a polite farewell (without sweeping the floor with my cap) and left. And this time, I promise you, the pitiful Mister Piktopek left the house of Morchiev, Morchiev & Sons for the last time . . .

In six months' time, when assistant manager Krokody thinks he is recalling the scene (and, in reality, he will merely be recalling his own petty dreams and the squalid aspirations of his soul), he will be able to say that the straw hat (he will probably say "the skimmer" or "the archbishop's hat") left the premises without demanding his due.

Besides, so stupid, useless, and slow did I appear in my former employers' recollections (recollections so fragile, so close to outright mirage, that they had ceased to recognize me as soon as I had changed headgear) that I had already reached the conclusion that there was no due there for me to demand.

My friend had dreamed up that whole fable about paid leaves of absence and wage increases in order to make me accept the help he wished to give me, seeing me in a condition that excited his brotherly sympathy, if not his pity.

Anxious to provide me with the ideal conditions for a retreat and meditation that would open me to the truth of myself (which is precisely what did occur, and the transformation partially explained the failure of the staff at Morchiev, Morchiev & Sons to recognize me), he had sought first of all to free my spirit from material concerns. It was his own money he had put in my pay envelopes at the end of each month (so it was hardly surprising that he had refused to take them back), and in the process he had ruined himself. I had been living off him all right!

All was now quite clear. As sharply defined as a figure in a geometry textbook. However, I doubted whether Miss Maria Wakhelyana was sufficiently imbued with the spirit of mathematics to concur with this particular theorem. On this point I was right.

To give her her due, she heard me through to the end. But by the time I had finished—her eyes reduced to mere slits in a face puffy from overindulgence in sweetmeats—she looked like a tiger about to spring on its prey.

"I knew it! I knew it!" she rasped. "You thought you were fooling me with your stupid lies, did you, you cunning little rat?" She raised a threatening palm. "Well, there's been enough joking, Mister Ghichka. I'm going to ram your Mister Crocodiles and all the others down your throat! Hand it over, you scummy bastard—now!"

"But—"

Grabbing my lapels, she hissed into my face, "Want me to search you? Want me to shake you until your shriveled balls fall off? Want me to cut you in little bits?"

Feverishly, I turned out my pockets, unlaced my shoes, and handed her my coat so that she could see there was nothing hidden inside the lining.

She snatched it and used it to rain blows on my head and shoulders.

"What have you done with it, swine?" she shrieked. "Where have you hidden it? You've stashed it somewhere in town, haven't you, with one of your whores? You filth! And I can just starve, is that it? Is that what you're hoping? You've shoved my money up some old whore's backside and put a lock and key on it, you thieving scum!"

She was really very angry and, occupied as I was with parrying the violent swipes she was aiming at me with my coat, I could utter nothing in my defense. Suddenly she hurled the coat from her and stood looking at me with grim pleasure, lips curled back from her teeth.

"I know!" she said. Pointing with her chin at Karl, she set her fists on her hips. "You've drunk it all away with that clown there, the maniac with four feet and a tail!"

"But," I ventured, raising my arms to protect my eyes, "he was with you all the time, Miss Maria Wakhelyana."

She exploded.

"Did you think I hadn't noticed? Perhaps you think it's easy for me to share my house with a zoo? How could I help seeing your little roommate, you tell me that! When he's not staring at doorknobs, he's burrowing into my skirts and making cow's eyes at me while he plays with his dick!"

"He's just copying me," I said pleadingly. "He's just trying to replace me so that you'll feel less alone . . . "

"My poor little Ghichka!" she cackled. "You could never be as expressive as that! Your face is as soft as another part of your body I could mention!"

"Some people think I look like Karl," I murmured humbly.

"What you look like is the shithouse window!" she screamed, embedding the tip of her pump in my shin.

Perhaps, by being gentle and mild, I might have hoped to patch things up. But the monkey, moved by some mysterious impulse, chose to imitate my spouse's gesture, except that it was her shin he aimed at. And since he had no pump to protect his foot, we were soon all three rolling on the kitchen tiles, moaning and clutching our ankles.

When Miss Maria Wakhelyana got up and realized that she was limping and that the monkey was limping in identical fashion, she screamed like a wounded animal; tearing at her hair (which had come undone and was hanging around her face), she cried out in tragic tones that she would not go on being aped by an ape.

But when I, too, had calmed down and approached (also with a limp) to console her, she began to beat her head against the wall.

For more than a week, she did not address a single word to me. The tasty little dishes I cooked for her splashed right back onto my shirtfront. She fed herself exclusively on Turkish delight and watched with a martyred air as Karl and I limped about.

The monkey pointed at her and then, with a wink, placed a finger on his lips. I was not sure what he was trying to tell me . . .

On May 9 to the day, having emptied a generous helping of noodles Parmesan into my pants (she had first unbuckled my belt), Miss Maria Wakhelyana sat down on the sofa, looked me straight in the eye, and said very calmly, "Very well. Since you refuse to support your own wife with the money that belongs to her as much as to you—more than to you, in fact, since it's my beloved Benazar Folykhulo's money—there are others who will be only too glad to take care of her."

"But Miss Maria Wakhelyana," I whimpered, "you know very well that everything Zebana . . . Kukulo left me is yours as well!"

"Really?" she said coldly. "And why should I believe that?"

"Because I say so, dear Miss Maria Wakhelyana! I, Ghichka Piktopek, your slave!"

She sniffed, not bothering to conceal her contempt.

"The word of a drunkard and a whore chaser!"

"You can take everything right now, Miss Maria Wakhelyana! I will help you if you like!"

"Of course! And give you a good excuse for sending me to jail!"

"But . . . "

"Stop bleating, you ninny! One animal is quite enough around here!"

"That is true, Miss Maria Wakhelyana, forgive me!"

"Never! Swine!"

"Yes, yes, you are right, Miss Maria Wakhelyana!"

"Are you trying to cheat me again, Ghichka? Admit it!"

"I admit it, Miss Maria Wakhelyana! But you are wrong to think it. I swear on everything I hold most dear that whatever I have is yours!"

"What you hold most dear, Ghichka, is my money! The rest isn't worth the rope to hang you with!"

"Of course, naturally, Miss Maria Wakhelyana. But please accept that I am renouncing all my possessions in your favor. I would merely put it to you that the noodles may have been a little overcooked . . . "

"You're trying to get around me. I want an affidavit."

"You shall have one, Miss Maria Wakhelyana."

"Now, you Judas!"

"At once!"

"Then what are you waiting for, you excrescence?"

"Nothing. I am not waiting for anything, my love. Perhaps I'm a little slow-moving . . . "

"Slow-moving? You are a dawdler, Ghichka, you are a sluggard!"

"That is so, Miss Maria Wakhelyana . . . "

"You are a malingerer!"

"People have often said so."

"They didn't say nearly enough, Ghichka! You're loathsome! You exude slime!"

"I believe you are right."

"You ooze, Ghichka."

"I could not have expressed it better myself, Miss Maria Wakhelyana."

"A real snail."

"Yes."

"A slug."

"Yes."

"You are revolting."

"People have the urge to wipe me off."

"But they can't find a dirty enough rag!"

To be brief, I signed the affidavit.

Miss Maria Wakhelyana secreted it in her bodice.

The monkey went over to see where it had gone.

A fresh drama erupted.

Next day, we were all three walking normally again.

But Miss Maria Wakhelyana, seeing that we had stopped limping at the same time she had, decided we had started to make fun of her again.

She broke a broom handle across our backs.

I hurried out to buy another one at the Peszczynski Department Store before closing time.

She thanked me with a smile and at once splintered it on my skull.

She brandished the affidavit I had given her and threatened to make me sleep outside with the monkey. She insinuated that I slept with the monkey anyway, inside or out. The monkey kissed me on the mouth and put his hand on my crotch. It was not a tactful move.

Next day Miss Maria Wakhelyana brought home a soldier and told us he was to be her lover.

"At your command!" said the soldier, slapping his hand to his belt buckle. "Consider it done!"

And it was done, right before our eyes.

The monkey held the candle.

I shined his boots (the soldier's, I mean).

In the morning, at Miss Maria Wakhelyana's request, the soldier handed her a tidy sum of money. I took off my cap. The monkey handed him his saber, whose handle he had smeared with apricot jam.

"Ten thousand cannons, I'll not stand for this!" thundered the soldier.

He was right. Attempting to flatten the monkey with one telling punch, he missed and tumbled down the stairs. It took three men to pull his helmet off.

In the process they accidentally wrenched off both his ears. Surreptitiously, the monkey slipped them into Maria Wakhelyana's apron. She found them as she groped for a handkerchief to wipe the poor man's brow, and set up such a howling that a streetcar was derailed and crashed into the front window of the taxidermist Von Schmultz.

Karl took advantage of the mishap to seize a magnificent female chimpanzee with blue eyes that had been shaken from its shelf and propelled in our direction by the impact.

With his prize under his arm, he galloped back up the stairs. Miss Maria Wakhelyana called the police. The police fell upon her as one man.

And so it was that the monkey and I plumbed the depths of disgrace and, on the strength of a document I myself had endorsed, were driven from our refuge like low criminals. The monkey was even forced to return the chimpanzee's left foot, which he had tried to hide behind his back. With great regret, the police drove away in the paddy wagon they had brought for us, once it had been established that Miss Maria Wakhelyana, who still clutched her lover's ears in her hands, could not credibly claim to be a victim of our lewdness.

Outside in the street, the smoke from the accident had almost vanished in the radiant sunlight. Armed with a pot of glue, Von Schmultz was hopping along the gutter in pursuit of the shattered debris of a collection that had brought him fame throughout the hemisphere; stripped of all zest for life, he looked as if he would like to stuff himself.

The streetcar driver was begging the pardon of the famous virtuoso Blavacek, tall, lanky, and lost; at the age of forty-nine, acting on the advice of a fashionable psychoanalyst, he had taken the streetcar for the first time in his life, in the company of his mother, his aunts, and his twelve sisters, and was now looking gloomily at his left little finger, which was as broad as it was long.

Everywhere were ruin and desolation. But there was not a cloud in the periwinkle sky. From Turkey (or perhaps from the depths of Persia), a gentle breeze wafted in a hint of olives and doughnuts laced with a whiff of artemisia, of almonds, and of violets. In a room under the rooftops, someone with a clarinet was playing a waltz my father used to hum when he was alone and not trying to think up jokes but counting his white hairs one by one and looking like his own father, and his father's father, and like all the fathers of all the fathers of all men drowning in the open air.

At that moment (had Krazkoch been a seaport), the intricate rigging of tall ships fresh from the spice trade and the spellbinding tropics would have begun to creak and sway, and clouds of gulls would have brought in a taste of salt, of spreading sails, and of the open sea.

Karl handed me his cane. I gave him my hand, leaning sideways a little because he was shorter than me, and we strolled off together down the wreckage-strewn street. As if we were alone in the whole world. As if we were on a country road, in the dusty light of sunset, the time of day when hearts expand, when vows are unmade, when exhausted cities fall back on their foundations of mud and mortal desires and dream old dreams, dreams of islands, dreams of blue palm trees and of beginnings.

In any case, I honored my contract, taking with me only the clothes on my back and the piece of mirror with my friend's face preserved on it. Karl took his straw hat and cane. Wishing to avoid a squabble, I left Miss Maria Wakhelyana all that remained of the director's money.

What would have happened if I had started to haggle? Nothing less than the exposing of our dark little secret — namely, that I had had no right to promise my wife untrammeled enjoyment of an inheritance to which I myself had no legal claim. The surest consequence of that would have been to land all three of us in the slammer — which would not have mattered to me personally but which I was reluctant to impose on Karl (given the municipal plots against his person) any more than on Maria Wakhelyana, whose fragile constitution would have suffered from prolonged contact with damp straw and rats; it was said that the boldest among the latter would challenge you for possession not only of your shoes but of your toes.

However, we now had to earn our living during an economic crisis in a metropolis where many young people, unable to find steady work, were already resorting to vagabondage, begging, and petty crime.

Yet some of them had pockets bursting with impressive qualifications. At the high noon of their youth, they had flocked into rooms with creaking floorboards and the ageless pungency of chalk to grapple with questions about the locomotion of grasshoppers and the intimate thoughts of people who had been dead for thousands of years.

Many of the questions masked hidden snares, laid by waspish old men who had to be physically assisted on their doddering way to the podium. But these fine young people, reaping the rewards of unremitting labor and long sleepless nights, had emerged victorious from these battles of wits and been awarded parchments that made their illiterate parents (dressed for the occasion in their Sunday best) gape in awe.

Then these laureates, chests swelling, had nailed up their humble shingles in a back alley of the old quarter against a wall spattered with nightingale droppings, and fearlessly set out to conquer the world, becoming teachers' aides, secretaries to exiled one-armed men or to seasoned hardware merchants, bottle-stopper inventors, nightclub doormen, and critics of cinematographical works in little magazines read with passionate interest from cover to cover by students in Berne and Prague.

Were they aware that these were their salad days? For their luck had changed, and now they were out on the street, their only passport an obsolete degree nobody even bothered to look at.

Sometimes they could trade them to people less intelligent than they for the price of a schnapps, but the gullible were becoming more and more rare. And, even among those who might still have been tempted, many hesitated to try to pass themselves off as doctors of philosophy lest their companions in misery laugh them to scorn.

If former laureates of the Imperial University who had once carved themselves a place in our society were now wearing out the soles of their shoes in Krazkoch, what hope was there for a former accounting clerk dismissed as an obsequious cretin by his employers?

And, indeed, all my efforts to find work at this time led to humiliating failure.

Nobody wanted me. With no ceremony at all, they gave me to understand that a man applying for a job hand in hand with a monkey could scarcely expect to be taken seriously.

Many were so offended by Karl's mania for imitating their every gesture that they showed me the door before I was able to tell even a quarter of the lies I had concocted for them. As for those who listened a little longer, they took the trouble to help me physically through the door, pointing out that they did not like to be made fun of and that I could keep my fairy tales for my twin. What twin?

Our only consolation on these dark days came from God. I mean that the weather remained as kind as it could possibly be to the homeless. And, since I still had my winter coat, my muffler, and the cap my friend had given me, we were not too unhappy sleeping under the stars.

Toward the end of June, it occurred to me that we might have better luck if we went our separate ways in search of work.

But a major obstacle now loomed. While the monkey was incapable of speech, I myself was incapable of performing the tasks that, thanks to his mimic's skill, he had mastered.

Together we devised a plan for turning this handicap to our advantage. I would go alone to interview prospective employers. Then, if they accepted my application, Karl would trade on his resemblance to me (heightening the resemblance by various artifices) and turn up for my job. This arrangement had the added advantage of freeing me to seek work I might actually be capable of handling.

Three days later, at a moment's notice, Karl had replaced the assistant of an esteemed surgeon.

My companion's talents were immediately appreciated by the interns, nurses, nurses' aides, and orderlies in the department run by the peerless Professor Tubülho Balaghri. For the great man was the slave of an overriding obsession: It was forbidden for any patient, once put under the scalpel and sewn up by his hands, to die in his department.

"Postoperative mortality rate: zero!" he would thunder as he strode down the corridors, his cape (with his name embroidered in silver letters on the back) swirling in the terrified faces of his pupils.

He would dance with rage on the threshold. "Nobody dies in my department! Here people live — and damn the cost! There is no postoperative mortality rate, merely an exorbitant rate of surgical ineptitude — and that means you, you idle good-for-nothings!"

As soon as a postoperative case was ready to take leave of this world, Karl had him discreetly moved to a ward with less exacting standards. When the professor made his rounds, Karl assumed the absent patient's appearance as well as his place in bed.

It didn't matter which cot the monkey occupied: As soon as the professor appeared in the midst of his nervous entourage, he would bear down on Karl, arm outstretched, and bellow, "Just look at that one! Take a good look at that stalwart human specimen! Don't tell me he doesn't look better than when he came in!"

He would grab the chart attached to the foot of the bed.

"Lung cancer! Double perforation of the intestine, ablation of the spleen, amputation of the left leg and right testicle. My God, the man looks healthier than I do! Eight days' rest and he's about ready to go home! Well done, my friend! You are what I call a miracle of modern medicine. Keep it up! Keep it up!"

And he would sweep onward to heap insults on a woman patient whimpering because half her brain was missing, the cavity in her skull filled with a rolled-up ball of newspaper.

Karl was alone among the practitioner's lieutenants to find favor in his eyes. "The only one," he would roar, "who does things exactly the way I do!"

As a result, whenever his chief went hunting or attended, with sadistic joy, the funeral of a colleague's patient, the monkey was entrusted with performing his operations, some of which were extremely delicate.

He carried out the task with his usual skill and won the gratitude of all his associates, for, unlike the irascible professor, he felt no need to shower them with reproaches bloodier even than the operating room in which he practiced his art.

Karl would mime all this for me when we met in the evenings, first at the Salvation Army shelter and later on the fourth floor of the small windowless hotel behind the central railroad station (the station no longer exists, but in those days it was a major center for a thriving traffic in locomotive wheels; readers will recall that this trade was behind one of the worst scandals of the regime, ultimately costing Minister Zspachkha his portfolio).

The improvement in our finances had made it possible for us to move first into one, then into the other establishment.

Once more, we had enough to eat. Karl was no longer obliged to imitate a cash customer at the corner bakery, somehow managing to project the illusion of a five-penny coin to the cashier. We were even able to order proper meals, with chicken in gravy and baked potatoes, at the little restaurant frequented by cab drivers just behind the former palace of the dukes of Szpamn, plus all the beer we could drink. Karl, more moderate than I, would push his mug across to me as we quietly chatted.

My companion was now earning a respectable salary, plus his share for the mortal remains of the hospital stiffs. And I, too, had finally found myself a job.

I was walking past a big mustachioed man, clad in heavy tweeds despite the burning heat, who was hiring at the lower end of Prosper-Gouphion-Monitor Street. Sure that he would reject me, I was walking past with my eyes straight ahead when he speared me with the tip of his umbrella.

"You there, big fellow! Wanna make a buck?"

"Why, yes," I answered a little doubtfully.

"Then follow me."

He led me to the rear of a truck and lifted the tarpaulin.

A black-skinned person was crouched inside, rolling eyes as big as billiard balls beneath a peaked cap.

"Hey, Benedict," said the man. "This is the sucker. Give him an outfit and keep an eye on him: I'm not sure I like the looks of him."

The black tossed me a white coat of doubtful cleanliness, which the man helped me put on. Then he pulled out a hinged board with a sort of harness between the two panels.

I just had time to see that the board carried a poster back and front with foot-high letters: "ONLY YESTERDAY I WAS BALD. THIS MORNING, I USED GRO-ROOT LOTION."

"But I wasn't bald yesterday," I objected as the man adjusted the sandwich board on my neck and shoulders.

The black man flashed a razor before my eyes.

"You'll have bald tonsils," he promised cavernously, "if you go on asking questions!"

"Oh, fine!" I said. "What do I have to do, gentlemen?"

"Just take a little stroll," said the man. "See the other end of the street down there?"

I looked carefully in the direction he was pointing.

"Yes, I see it," I said finally.

"Great!" said the man. "Smart as a whip!" His assistant shrugged, but I gave no sign I had noticed. "Well, walk down there."

"I can manage that," I said. "I have often done it."

"He's a nitwit!" growled the black. "I don't like it."

The man looked testily at him.

"Mind letting me do my job, Benedict?"

The black's only response was to drop the tarpaulin over the rear of the truck and disappear from view. The man patted my cheek.

"Don't you worry, Jack! Don't worry about him!"

"My name is Ghichka," I said.

"Shut up, will ya?"

"I'm sorry," I said.

"You're welcome," he said. "Now then, you walk to the end of the street."

"You can count on me," I said.

"I told you to shut up."

"It just came out."

"Watch it!" he said.

"I'm sorry," I said.

"What did I tell you?" he said.

"That's true," I said.

"Well?" he said.

"I'm sorry," I said.

"Christ Almighty!" he said.

"Uh . . . no, that's not what I was going to say," I said.

"Are you doing this on purpose?" he said.

"No," I said. "I'm sorry."

"There's gonna be trouble!" he said. "I can feel it coming!"

"I'm listening," I said. "I'm only a beginner. I'm sor—"

"Benedict!" he yelled. "Get over here!"

"I walk to the end of the street," I said hastily, hoping to calm him down.

"That's right," he said with a worried expression. "And no tricks!"

"Rest assured," I said.

"You walk to the end of the street," he said, "and then . . ."

94

"And then?"

"You walk back."

"Very well," I said. "That's logical."

"I piss on your logic!" he said. "Get it?"

"Yes," I said. "You are quite right."

"I'm going to kill him!" he said.

"Go ahead," I said a little carelessly. "I shall tell no one."

"OK," he said, "OK." He seemed suddenly to have sunk into deep melancholy.

"There is no cause for anxiety," I said. "I can walk back up a street even quicker than I walk down it."

"I suppose so," he sighed. "I suppose so."

"You have no need to worry," I said. "What should I do next, please?"

He was gazing sightlessly about him.

"Walk back down again, I guess," he mumbled.

"And then?"

"Come back up."

"People are bound to notice."

"You think so?" he said.

Doubtless he had failed to consider this possibility, for a dejected look crossed his face. He waved his right thumb and index finger.

"How many fingers do I have?" he said.

"That depends," I said.

"Just what I expected," he said ruminatively. "Well, off you go, kid. If you see your shadow following you, don't worry too much, it probably couldn't get itself a seat at the movies."

"I shan't worry," I said. "I'm used to it."

Sorrowfully shaking his head, he propelled me out

into the human river flowing along the sidewalk. I had no idea what had triggered his sudden gloom.

However that may be, I walked until nightfall from one end of Prosper-Gouphion-Monitor Street to the other, ignoring the pains stabbing up from my feet to the roots of my nose, as well as the more or less witty sallies from other users of the public way.

"Something wrong with that there lotion!" shouted a barber from the doorway of his shop across the street. "You're even balder than my mother-in-law's asshole."

At one point I noticed that the man in tweeds and his acolyte, in wigs hanging down to their knees, had set up a little stand on the other side of the Crossroads of the Clock and were offering passersby small phials filled with bluish liquid.

"Here's your buck," said the man as he unstrapped my harness five or six hours later. He had recovered his aplomb. "You're not so bad after all. You look such a dope all those idiots out there believe you. If you want another buck, Jack, meet us tomorrow morning, eleven o'clock, corner of Khalabarhy Street and the Street of the Blessed Pontiffs."

In other words, slap in the middle of the Kristophory quarter. My feet felt like raw steak, but it would be a chance to get a glimpse of Miss Maria Wakhelyana's entrancing form. At ten o'clock I was already waiting for the truck.

This time the sign said, "ONLY YESTERDAY I WAS A DRUNKEN WRECK. THIS MORNING I STARTED TAKING MARSUPIAL MILK AND HAVE ALREADY FOUND A JOB."

The job in question seemed very much like yesterday's, except that this time my patrolling was constantly interrupted by strangers eager to shake my hand and sometimes to slip a coin into it.

In front of the basilica, my associates were offering little phials of some pale brown liquid, but Miss Maria Wakhelyana failed to appear; when I picked up my dollar at the end of the day, I could only stand there fingering it stupidly, the corners of my mouth pulled down to bite back the tears.

Next day, near the Gunpowderworks, I offered the following information to the public: "ONLY YESTERDAY I DID NOT BELIEVE IN THE VIRTUES OF STARCH-ESSENCE VIRILITY OIL. THIS MORNING I CAN BARELY WALK."

I did not need to try hard to lend credibility to the second part of the message: I had the impression that my shoes no longer encased anything but a shapeless mush of cartilage, of broken bones, and of flesh crushed in a rolling mill.

Not far away, the man in tweeds and the tonsil shaver were frantically distributing little phials of colorless liquid to an eager throng of customers.

That night they decided to cut me in on their profits and called me by my right name for the first time. Beneath their rough exteriors, in fact, they were worthy people; my only regret is that I have not met more people half as human as they were.

Meanwhile, Karl was consolidating his position at the hospital.

The whole surgical department now swore by him. Patients adored him, knowing that with him around they could die in peace without fear of being taxed with malingering or ingratitude. And the professor himself, after watching him in action, was considering appointing Karl his successor when he retired.

He had already brought him into his research activities, focusing on the use of a sardine-can opener to open up the skull—an innovation that would incontestably represent a giant step forward in techniques of emergency trepanning at picnic sites.

My beloved primate would certainly have ended his days in the uniform of a member of the Institute had I not, in a fit of carelessness, committed an unpardonable error.

On August 23 I was walking down the sidewalk outside the Tubülho Balaghri Hospital, wearing my white coat.

My step was light and there was a smile on my lips, for, in another three days, the monkey and I would be deserting our windowless hotel for a delectable villa in the southwestern suburbs, which an old lady had agreed to rent to us for a modest sum . . .

How could I have guessed that on that very morning the professor who had taken Karl under his wing would erupt from the operating room like a whirlwind, having just learned from his anesthetist (may the devil cut out his tongue!) that not fifty feet from the hospital they were burying a family that had perished en masse under the scalpel of his most hated rival?

Ripping off his mask and tossing at my friend the screwdriverlike implement with which he had been probing his patient's eyesockets, he rushed out. "You finish, Mister Ghichka!" he shouted as he left. "Pry his eyes out of his head if need be, but remember—postoperative mortality rate: zero!"

Zero, the monkey acknowledged, making a circle with thumb and forefinger and snuffing out the patient's last breath with the palm of his other hand. His chief was already gone . . .

In fact, he was already—but how could I have foreseen it? how could I have foreseen it?—within reading distance of the poster on my back, which announced to the clear summer air (I had barely glanced at it): "ONLY YESTERDAY I WAS DOOMED TO PERISH ON THE OPERATING TABLE. THIS MORNING, THANKS TO THE MAGUS BEN BALIBORA'S ELIXIR, I AM CURED AND FEEL TWENTY YEARS YOUNGER."

The worst might have been averted had the professor not been persuaded by my white coat and general appearance that I was his own assistant. He could never have believed Karl capable of such a betrayal. It was as if the earth had opened up under his feet.

The manner in which the madman hurled himself upon me, with the full intention of making me swallow my poster, still causes me horrible nightmares today (not to mention the stabbing pains that torture my jaws whenever it begins to rain). And I have to admit that Benedict did not help matters by slitting my attacker's throat from ear to ear.

The great practitioner had been a childhood friend of the mayor, to whom he had frequently loaned his hoop; a cousin of the racing cyclist Bornjiak (also known as Mirza), three-time winner of the backbreaking Bhrnmu hillclimb; president of N.A.S.N.P.M. (National Association of Surgeons for a Negative Postoperative Mortality) and of the Brotherhood of Calf's-Head Fanciers (whose annual proceedings in the upstairs banqueting suite of the Crowned Hart Inn traditionally culminated in riotous feasting and the election amid sly winks and cheers of Miss Calf's Head); honorary member of several civilian and paramilitary associations; and a staunch supporter of the government of the day, whatever its leanings. His fame in Krazkoch had long since transcended his professional prestige. His wife could walk, head held high, into any grocer's in town and be greeted by name and served the best-quality produce at the fairest prices.

While alive, the famous doctor had wielded powerful

influence and had not hesitated to use it. Now, even though his throat had been slit like a barnyard fowl's, he was no less to be feared than in life. On the contrary! For us the only hope of safety lay in flight.

My associates needed no telling: Jettisoning phials, stand, and razor, they leapt into their truck and took off like the wind before I even had a chance to embrace them.

Two hours later, Karl and I — he had emerged from the hospital to investigate the uproar, and I was watching for him from an open-air urinal — packed our meager belongings and stole out of town by the most round-about route.

At Sztolgha we took the bus, boarding separately in order to throw off suspicion. As that terrible day was drawing to a close, we got off at the terminus in Zoparice, deep in the farm country.

The monkey booked a room at the Hotel Medusa while I went to the Golden Carp. The sheets were immaculately clean, and, at the bottom of the chamber pot, there was a large accusing eye. The owners of these two hostelries nursed a hereditary hatred for each other; all night long they hurled insults back and forth through the closed shutters, lowering their voices only when they chanced to recall our presence in their rustic madhouse.

But, even if they had kept totally silent, I doubt whether either of us would have been able to sleep. We had left too many memories, too many ashes, and too much debris behind us. We had borne too many regrets and too much blighted love into exile with us. If the director of the Kirchenstahl Gardens ever returned from his wanderings, what hope had he of finding our trail across this wasteland of plowed fields and forlorn pastures?

And in my case there was the added torture of being sundered forever from Miss Maria Wakhelyana. For she was not the kind of young lady to venture into the countryside, and recent events in the capital had banished Karl and me from there for the rest of our days.

Oh, I had not forgotten that she had turned me out of my house, out of her sight, out of her life. Passion had not made me so blind that I imagined she might still want me, even if I laid treasures at her feet. (She would take the treasures, give me a paper to sign, and hasten to the window to summon the police.) But it was one thing to be kept at a distance by her adored hand, and quite another to endure an exile so final that I could no longer hope to catch even a glimpse of her—or at the very least of some young woman with whom it might just be possible to confuse her . . .

At the crack of dawn we set our feet on the path of misery and exile again. Using varied means of transport, including a Dutch barge, we put as many miles as possible (every one of them a torture) between Krazkoch and ourselves.

We traveled for three whole days, not stopping until the chalky loam and grim, ungiving soil of the North had snuffed out the last exhalations of the happier, more generous South, where the earth leaves a warm moist imprint on the palm of your hand.

Everything around us cried out that we had entered purgatory. And it was here that we must henceforth live.

Live how? On what? My weedy physique disqualified me for work in the fields. Furthermore, we were afraid that Karl would be unable to hide his true identity from the peasantry. Tillers of the soil live closer to nature and see things more clearly than city folk; persuading them that sow's ears were silk purses would be no easy task.

With few exceptions, the villages were tiny hamlets. Most people lived on isolated farms at great distances from one another, as if everyone expected the worst of his neighbor. We quickly learned that courting a girl in these parts was much more perilous than prowling the jungle at night or hunting the saber-toothed tiger armed only with a cat-o'-nine-tails would be in other places.

We invested our last pennies in an ancient motorcycle and sidecar; on it we rode from farm to farm in search of work.

We had agreed beforehand that we would lay our cards on the table at once, so as not to undermine our credibility with the rustics from the outset.

"Well, now," I would say to the master of the house, "would you like the monkey to imitate someone for you?"

Usually, after giving it some thought, the man would decline our offer. We made it a rule never to insist. People in the countryside are extremely wary. We had to give them time to get used to us.

I would keep on smiling through their refusals.

"Very well!" I would say. "Forgive the intrusion. Another time perhaps . . . "

I would leap nimbly into the saddle and off we would go, waving and being very careful not to run over the poultry.

Some of them wanted to know how much it would cost.

I had my plan worked out.

"Nothing for the first imitation!" I would say heartily.

"A free sample, if you will. Can't afford to buy a pig in a poke these days, can you?"

They readily agreed. Huddling together in a corner of the farmyard while I carefully parked the sidecar, they would ponder the role they wanted my companion to play. Sometimes they consulted me.

"Whoever you like!" I would say reassuringly. "No restrictions! Any person living or dead, private or public . . . "

I had worked my spiel out to the letter.

"Hmm," the man would say doubtfully. "I don't know . . . My wife's aunt, maybe?"

"And why not yours?" his spouse would retort. "He'd find it a lot easier!"

They usually arrived at a compromise. Nine times out of ten, a neighbor or his wife. Depending on the case, Karl would stick a cloth cap on the back of his head or knot a scarf under his chin.

"Yes, yes," chorused the spectators, "that's him (her), all right!"

They did not seem too enthusiastic, though.

"If that's all there is to it, we could just as easily have had him (her) come over in person," the wife would grumble.

"Aren't you satisfied with the likeness?" I would ask, more confidently than I felt.

"It's not the likeness, no," growled the farmer. "On the contrary."

"On the contrary?"

He spat a blackish stream of saliva on the dungheap.

"What's it to us to see someone we can see whenever we want to?" he asked.

"Well—" I began.

"Someone we see too often, you mean!" his wife broke in. "If you ask me, I could do without seeing them at all . . . "

"What about someone you've never seen but would like to?" I asked.

"Who might that be?" asked the man, scratching an eyebrow.

"If it's someone we don't know, how can we tell if it's a good likeness?" his wife objected.

"We guarantee it," I said.

"The way a robber proclaims his innocence at the foot of the gallows," intoned an elder.

"What if the monkey imitated me?"

"Certainly not," they chorused.

"Listen," I said soothingly, "Karl will do you the Reichschancellor, and it won't cost you a penny!"

"None of that here!" the man said flatly. "You one of them there agitators, or what?"

"Shall I get the gamekeeper, Dad?" asked the grown-up son.

"Don't trouble yourselves," I said with a smile. "Forgive the intrusion. Another time perhaps."

I leapt nimbly into the saddle and off we went, waving. But, if a cow had happened to be in our way, I would have run right over it rather than delay our retreat a fraction of a second.

All this, of course, did nothing to fatten our wallets. And now an early autumn was tightening its grip on the hedgerows, just like last year. And winter was looming. And hunger was twisting our insides.

A terrible autumn. A lethal autumn. The rains began; it was as if someone had left for the ball and forgotten to turn off the faucet.

One day the rain fell straight down, the next it slanted, but it was always the same rain, cold, endless, biting.

I, who had never been able to do anything with my hands, was forced to hammer together a frame that we fitted over our vehicle to shelter us from the elements.

Sometimes the rain seemed to be mingled with a colorless, translucent soup that made it look like melting sherbet; soon we would have snow to contend with.

The snow did indeed come and, almost at once, it assailed us savagely.

Our nights were endless calvaries. We shivered in each other's arms, praying for day to come. But, when day came, it merely prolonged the night by adding to it a hint of pallor that was scarcely an improvement.

Nevertheless, since it was day, we made each other believe there was new hope. I kicked the engine into life; it was an exhausting task, but at least it pumped a little life into my numb body.

We set off down sunken roads, stopping constantly to scrape off the mud that clogged us and our machine.

Crisscrossing remote country areas, we did our best to avoid populated zones, where they would be waiting for us with guns in their hands. There was no direction to our wandering; we went on only because we had nowhere to go.

Meanwhile, despite all our efforts at thrift, our resources were dwindling to nothing. Soon we were living on a frugal diet of black bread washed down with a mouthful of water made by melting three handfuls of snow in an old tin can. To save gasoline, we forced ourselves to make more and more frequent stops in spite of the terrible cold.

The day came when we half-filled the gas tank and realized that we would not be able to do it again.

That same day, in a dingy hostelry where we had stopped to trade our last coins for a hot drink, come what may, we learned that war had just been declared.

On whom? On Moldavia, I imagined. It would have been insane to attack the Russians or the Germans, and Liechtenstein was much too far away. Whereas the Moldavians seemed ideal antagonists in an armed conflict, as if God had created them just for that. If Moldavians even imagined they saw the glint of a knife through the bushes, they would huddle together with shrill screams, raising their arms as high as they could; and, if one of them ever got it into his head to clean his rifle, his neighbor would be sure to receive the bullet between his eyes.

Tottering, staggered by the terrible news, we drained our grogs and hastened out of that pigsty, our pockets weighed down with emptiness.

Outside, the storm was raging and our vehicle looked strangely lopsided. While we had been inside trying to build up our pitiful strength, someone had stolen the front wheel . . .

It was the end of our wanderings. There was nothing left to do but lay ourselves down in this powder, so reminiscent of the dust of centuries and of unrequited loves, of the ineluctable crumbling of human dreams, and abandon ourselves to the only dream that never ends.

But it was not to be.

This seemingly fatal stroke turned out to be the first smile destiny had deigned to bestow on us for a long, long time. Without this war, without this theft and the consequent delay in our departure from the village, we would already have been halfway to the grave; at the eleventh hour, fortune had granted us a fresh reprieve.

A wheelwright off to join his regiment gave us a big wheel from a garden barrow; he even helped us fit it to the motorbike's front fork. It was an unconventional arrangement, but at least we could move if we kept our speed down.

We did not move very far.

Twenty yards from the hostelry, a man leapt from a house and stood in our path, arms outspread to bar our way. Anticipating trouble, I tried to steer around him, but the motor stalled.

"Are you the man with the monkey?" he asked Karl.

I hesitated to reply. I knew the malevolence of these

peasants too well by now to throw myself trustingly into the lion's maw. Beside me, though, Karl showed no alarm. He was even eyeing the stranger in a friendly manner, two fingers raised to his forehead as was his custom in the presence of a potential customer.

"You're from the city," the man went on. "You must know lots of things we don't even dream of here. About this war, for instance . . . It seems to me wars are always started by our betters, by the big wheels . . . You must know some of the big wheels. Come on in, my wife's just cooked a venison pie. Just park your putt-putt in the shed over there. Brrr, not a warm day, is it? You'll be much better off indoors than riding all over the countryside, particularly this late in the day. Look, it's already getting dark!"

When we met again, he was on his threshold on the other side of the farmyard. He took the hat and cane that had become my showman's uniform.

"Let me have that! Come in and make yourselves comfortable!" he said heartily.

He led us into a big dining room smelling of furniture polish and of rustic abundance.

Huge logs burned in the hearth, casting lambent splashes of purple deep into the shadows and over the spotless dark wood furniture.

When I saw the lead-paned windows I felt something tear deep within me. I barely had time to bite into my lower lip. My God! My God!

There was also a girl too shy to look up at us; she sat in a corner, her hands folded in her apron.

"This is Cendrella, my daughter," the man said.

Blushing, she made a touchingly clumsy curtsy.

Then I looked more closely at her and realized that she was pretty, which for me is better than being beautiful; for, in my eyes, beauty—what people call real beauty—always has an intimidating side, even an inhuman one. Prettiness is rather like childhood prolonged; beauty is like the approach of death. When people tell me that such and such a woman is a perfect beauty, I see someone whose nose is too long and whose eyes are a hundred centuries old. I get away before she can even open her mouth, afraid that it will give off a whiff of the tomb. And Cendrella was a pretty name, a name that made you long for spring and for something blue in the hollow of your hand. I believe I smiled.

At that moment the mistress of the house bustled in bearing an enormous soup bowl with an odor subtler than all the perfumes of Araby.

"Welcome, gentlemen!" she beamed. "The meat pie isn't quite done, but here's something to help you kill the time! Cendrella, my sweet, don't just sit there. Pour our guests a drop of the liquid gold. It's a late wine; I think you'll like it."

The man raised his glass.

"To your health!"

"Well, now," he said, after we had polished off the last crumb of dessert (a juicy cherry pie). "So it's war again, eh? What's it all about this time? What's happening behind the scenes? There's never smoke without a fire! They always show us the war itself, but what are they hiding from us? Cendrella, take your leave of these gentlemen, will you? This isn't a conversation for young ladies."

I rose so quickly to say good-bye to the girl that I

knocked my chair over. Cendrella was barely able to stifle a giggle. Her parents pursed their lips disapprovingly.

But they need not have worried. I fully realized that she was not laughing at me. She was just amused, that was all. It is the privilege of youth and innocence. Whereupon I myself began to laugh. No doubt about it, she enchanted me, this young lady with her little-girl ways. And her hand was one of the softest and whitest I had ever held. I wanted to hold it forever; which is why, fearing that it might be noticed, I let it go so abruptly it looked as if I had been bitten.

Cendrella had to hurry out to hide another outburst of merriment. How exquisite she was! An icy breath swept my heart as she crossed the threshold and disappeared (or perhaps I should say "evaporated," she was so light and quick-moving).

"So?" the father resumed (for this whole episode had lasted barely three seconds). "What's behind it all?"

I, too, had a question to ask, but I asked it only of myself: How could I explain to him that I knew much less of war than he did? He would not have believed me. All his prejudices conspired to make him believe that I, a city dweller, had the ear of politicians and the confidence of military planners.

What good would it do to tell him of my indifference — indeed, my repugnance — to everything going on outside me, to everything that inflamed the mob, a species that has always been more alien and hostile to me than hyenas or snakes? He would feel insulted, offended, deliberately misled after all his hospitality toward us. My chances of regaling this man with well-informed speculation about a conflict whose belligerents I could not begin to identify were no greater than my

111

chances of stumbling on the formula for squaring the circle, a secret that has eluded great minds for centuries.

I glanced at my dear Karl for help. Lord God! As if a monkey could possess insight into the labyrinthine world of international relations!

And yet, before my startled eyes, he pushed back his chair, took up a position before our host, and launched into a succession of pantomimes that plunged me deeper and deeper into bewilderment.

But not the farmer.

"Oh?" he exclaimed, starting on his chair. "Really? Oh! No? Is that so? I don't believe it! What? Good God, what swine! Who'd have thought it! Then what? Ahah! Ahaha! Well, well! What a mess!"

I could not have been more nonplussed if Karl had suddenly treated us to his mime of the mating dance of the lesser tufted bandersnatch.

The man was waving his arms.

"Wait! Wait! You have to tell all this to the others! If I told them, they'd just laugh at me. I won't be a minute!"

He ran from the room. His wife chose that moment to pour us two generous tumblers of old applejack. I dared not even look my companion in the face: I had the painful impression that I was sitting opposite a monkey I did not know.

Next minute the dining room was full of closed-faced men staring at the animal with almost unbearable intensity.

They all leaned forward so as not to miss one of Karl's gestures. I, too, watched him as closely as I could, but I'll be damned if I understood one iota more than the first time around.

When it was over, the men walked slowly away, their faces thoughtful. Our farmer saw them to the door, shaking hands warmly and methodically all around.

"Be back here tomorrow at the same hour, neighbors," he told them. "The situation will doubtless have evolved by then, and Mister Karl will bring us up to date. Today he had to put his report together at a moment's notice, improvising all the way, but by tomorrow we'll have had time to think about it a little: I promise you things will be very much better organized. Tell the neighbors, and bring as many as you can. Everyone will be welcome: With half the planet hurtling toward destruction, the time for petty squabbles among ourselves is over!"

By next evening all the furniture had been pushed back against the walls. Chairs and benches had been arranged twelve rows deep around the center of the room.

With Cendrella's help, the man had brought down from the attic an old marionette theater with a red velvet curtain. He had put a fresh coat of paint on it and set it up five feet from the front row.

He had spent the rest of the day rounding up various props from neighbors' houses (helmets from the last war converted into flowerpots, faded tunics, battered trumpets), drawing up plans, sticking little flags onto outdated road maps, and covering billboards with illustrations torn from almanacs and books given as prizes at school (here, the Diet; there, a gunboat shelling Foochow; beyond, a rolling landscape sewn with small white crosses).

At the appointed hour the neighbors trooped in and took their seats. The farmer wound up a gramophone and flooded the room with strident martial music. As the last bars faded, he gave a discreet sign, and Cendrella, from her hiding place under the heavy folds of the tablecloth, tugged at the complex mechanism that opened the red curtain.

There, in center stage, was Karl against a backdrop depicting (if the reader will be so indulgent) a Prussian infantryman shitting into a grandfather clock with an expression of bestial contentment.

The audience gave a shudder of horror. Quite unmoved, my companion removed the picture and replaced it with a view of an even more satisfied-looking Uhlan spearing babies on the tip of his lance.

In the audience men rose, their faces white and drawn. But the monkey seemed as impervious to these boiling reactions as if his audience were invisible.

A brightly colored general staff map appeared as if by magic on the spot where, mere seconds before, the Uhlan had been abandoning himself to his foul activities.

Now Karl parodied a whole litany of bizarre characters, distinguishing them one from the other by skillful recourse to the props with which he had been supplied. But they all looked like insane-asylum inmates to me.

"Good heavens!" cried the peasants. "The king of the Belgians!"

"Damnation! Bulgarian cavalry!"

"But that's Joseph Stalin! The Little Father of All the Russias . . . He gets fatter every day, that swine!"

"No, no—that's his double, the poor devil who gets stabbed by assassins and has to taste his soup for him."

"You're right, by God! The real one has a thicker mustache."

"He never appears in public anymore. Perhaps he's dead."

"Well, in that case, the double was the other one. Maybe they poisoned his soup."

"Hey! See the little one in the corner there?"

"The top hat?"

"That's the one! It's the emperor of Japan!"

"He's in it as well?"

"My God, how yellow he is!"

"Sweet Jesus! It's the wickedness in him coming out!"

"And his eyes! How could you ever guess what he's thinking with a face like that?"

"We haven't heard the last of those little vermin!"

"Yes, and we'll be the ones who'll suffer!"

Crouched behind the theater's cardboard backdrop, never missing a cue, our farmer handed the monkey illustrations, headgear, lists of statistics, and Dantesque representations of naval disasters or of infantrymen disemboweling one another at the bottom of trenches.

"This war's the worst of them all!" the man next to me muttered in an awed voice. "Good God, the last was just child's play!"

Onstage, Karl was pounding a whole regiment of lead soldiers with a frying pan.

Night after night the show went on. The audience, its ranks soon swollen by women and children, began to organize itself. People brought food along. While (thanks to the monkey's talent) unidentified bands of men pegged their captives down on red-ant nests in the jungles of Malaya, the audience passed bottles around. Wits and hecklers began to make themselves heard. "Happy eating!" someone shouted to the insects.

There were two intermissions. But Karl would remain at his post, miming the virtues of the farmer's cider, which the latter's wife and daughter brought round in great wicker baskets, charging first twenty cents a bottle, then fifty, then one hundred. This was, of course, rather expensive, but people told each other that you didn't get the chance to drink such fine homemade cider every day.

In truth, our hosts very soon exhausted their own supplies and were now filling their bottles with commercial cider purchased for ten cents a quart at the village grocer's. The joke was that the grocer (whose family invariably arrived over an hour in advance to grab the best seats) always guzzled this swill down with gusto, proclaiming to all and sundry that nothing could compare with the real farm-grown stuff, the product of a man's own hands and of the love in his heart.

I never even dreamed of wetting my lips with it. I preferred to watch Cendrella as she moved gracefully among the spectators. The mere sight filled my cup, satisfying my needs beyond all hope. If I could have had that picture permanently before my eyes, I should have been able to go without drink, without food, even without breathing. I begged heaven not to let her suspect these bold thoughts of mine. Luckily for me, her duties as cider vendor and stagehand left her no time even to notice my presence. But I pitied her for being so shamelessly used, or rather exploited, by her father.

One day our host drew the monkey aside.

"You know, Mister Karl," he said, "all this slaughter, all this shelling, all these mass executions, they're a bit . . . how shall I put it? Well, not very edifying! And it gets pretty dull, no doubt about that. People are getting bored. It's all too grim. Maybe you could perk up their spirits with a French cancan number? What do you think?"

I have to acknowledge that, commercially speaking, it was not a bad idea. The French cancan seemed to heighten the gentlemen's thirst considerably, and the ladies screamed and cheered.

Our host took the monkey aside again.

"You know, Mister Karl, having fun is fine, but we shouldn't neglect the spiritual side . . . "

Late at night, with the bleachers three-quarters empty and accompanied by the soft snores of the few who had stayed, my companion skillfully juggled the dynasties of ancient Egypt, mimed tuna fishing off Iceland, or showed the infant Mozart trying to scale a piano stool much too high for him—a truly tear-jerking tableau.

His twenty-four-episode series on the manufacture of the Afghan whistle (whose sound is uncannily like that of an ordinary whistle) earned him the village school-master's congratulations.

Mine, too, for I did not want him to think that I was indifferent to his efforts.

Indifferent, no. But a stranger to them, alas! more and more.

It was not my fault. Nor his fault. But there it was: We, who had been on the point of death together, were now living in the same house without much more contact than two hotel residents who had arrived separately and who now met by chance from time to time in the vestibule or the dining room.

Each of us had his own room. Karl was the darling of the whole household. I seemed a mere parasite. By the time I rose, with nothing to do but kick my heels in the yard until it was time to eat, he had already been up for hours, rehearsing his parts, dreaming up the latest news from the front, pondering the best way of making Kantian logic accessible to a popular audience, helping our farmer to furbish the sets, establishing figures and statistics, and so on.

There was scarcely enough time in the day for him to prepare the evening's performance, and I was of no use to him, being totally ignorant in all these fields. My presence at his side would merely have been a burden to him.

And, since he had decided to save time by taking his meals "on the job" — that is to say, in the workshop where I never set foot — the only chance I ever had of seeing him was at his performances, which now began at seven o'clock sharp with local news and retrospective coverage of the Olympic Games, and carried on until well after midnight, closing with "Thoughts on the Contemporary Novel," a series nobody watched but for which everybody professed the highest regard, protesting whenever its cancellation was proposed.

Karl was not withdrawing from me. I was not withdrawing from Karl. Nevertheless, we were separated by a gulf that daily yawned wider. Karl on one side of the red curtain. Me on the other. And, once the curtain rose, our separation was even more marked. For my companion was projected into the luminous solitude of a genius largely beyond my understanding; whereas I was absorbed and ingested by the anonymous mass of those who, sitting in semidarkness, contemplated the fruit of that genius with a passivity that can by no stretch of the imagination be compared with the anarchic soarings and swoopings of love.

Even then, my admiration counted for less than theirs, since I did not understand (or understood only dimly) the value of Karl's tableaux, depicting as they did events shaking the planet and not the events of everyday existence.

I sensed that I had seen the last of the days when, staring into Karl's eyes, I had the illusion of seeing myself in a mirror. All this brandishing of bayonets and shakos that now absorbed him held no meaning for me. I would not have recognized myself in them even if (like the friendly wheelwright of this same village) I had been forced to put on a uniform and charge into the bullets like everyone else.

I watched Karl, sitting framed in his box. I missed not a hair's twitch of his expressions, not one of the often imperceptible movements that activated the different parts of his body. I could shout just as loudly as everyone else in the room, "Hey! That's Churchill! Maurice Chevalier! Haile Selassie! Fat Mussolini, boooo! Get rid of him!" but the tribulations of this little world did not seem any less aberrant, trivial, and above all unreal.

But wasn't there, if not an interest, at least some *sense* for me in all this tangle? Could nobody explain it to me? I was floundering helplessly.

Where were the Moldavian hordes in all this? I had been expecting one war, and a completely different one had developed—and one, moreover, that made not an ounce of sense. It was as if everyone from horizon to horizon were trying to add his own personal turmoil to the universal apocalypse.

I kept my eyes on the monkey. He never stopped. He went from general to general, from continent to continent, and, wherever he went, he unearthed eccentricities unworthy of a carnival night.

As if they weighed a ton, my hands dropped heavily to the sides of my chair. A thought came to me: "If this is, as it seems to be, the mirror of the world, is there any room anywhere for my own reflection?"

Having said these words to myself, I was instantly flooded by a wave of bitterness and desolation. Choking on my sorrow, I seized my throat in both hands and leapt from my seat. I felt more deprived of my own person than a ghost must feel. Rushing blindly from the room, I climbed up to my bedroom and threw myself full-length on the bed, sobbing violently.

Much later (or perhaps it was only a few minutes—how can you be sure when your despair is so complete?), I heard a noise in the room. Light as a cloud, a hand fell on my shoulder. An angel's voice whispered, "You know, Mister Karl frightens me, too, sometimes!"

I turned my head. I dared to open an eye.

Cendrella's excellent young face was leaning over me.

I had not known that you can love so many times in your life. Every love is so enormous, so complete, so overwhelming that I did not believe such a thing possible. Unless I am what people sometimes call a man who wears his heart on his sleeve.

What matter, so long as it has given me more loving feelings than others enjoy? For no love is exactly the same as any that has gone before.

In love, all the feelings in the world visit your heart for the first and for the last time; that is why every single one of them gives you a sense of rebirth; that is why, in the most perfect love, your heart dies, they say, more than a thousand and one times; and that is why, in love (whether that love is extremely perfect or a little less so), your heart always stays young.

"Have you ever loved anyone else?" murmured Cendrella. "Tell me, Mister Ghichka. I want to know. I won't be angry, you know. Everything you have ever done seems good to me. And so does everything you ever will do."

My head was pillowed on her apron, in her parents' hayloft where we hid our love from the world. God in heaven! How tenacious love is! How often it returns to the attack, fugitive though it is . . .

"I have loved many, my sweetheart, but you are the first."

"How they must have loved you, Mister Ghichka, all those women! Oh, how I wish I could meet them!"

"They did not all love me, my sweetheart. And not all of them were women. You cannot say that your sister is a woman unless you are a little bit perverse. Mister Banez . . . well, anyway, someone you've never met, was a man, and he is dead. As for Karl, he's neither a man nor a woman, since he's a monkey."

"You love Mister Karl, Mister Ghichka?"

"As much as I love myself. It isn't much, and yet it's everything when you think that he's only an animal when all is said and done. But I love you more."

"More than the monkey?"

"Of course, my sweetheart. Don't be silly. I love you — period. That means more than everything, more than myself, more than more!"

"And . . . have you ever loved anyone else — period?"

"Well, you know, I'm wondering. There was Miss Maria Wakhelyana, of course, but that was a long time ago. She was different. Once I thought I loved her too much. But too much is like not enough. If you don't love the way you should, my sweetheart, you cannot love anyone properly. God wanted it that way."

"What was she like, Mister Ghichka, this Miss Maria Wakhelyana?"

"She was . . . she was the Madonna—except more life-like, of course."

"Sweet Jesus! How she must have loved you!"

"Of course she didn't! What makes you think so?"

"She was probably hiding it. A lot of girls are very shy, you know," she said, blushing deliciously.

"I suppose it's possible, my sweetheart. You know women's hearts better than I do."

"How could a woman not love you, Mister Ghichka?"

"Or vice versa. It's all so mysterious . . . "

"And you let her go?"

"In a way."

"You didn't try to make her stay?"

"No. We were married, you see. And I had signed the affidavit . . . "

"The affidavit? What affidavit, Mister Ghichka?"

"Oh, just an affidavit. Don't worry about it, my sweetheart! I've forgotten the whole sad business."

"Obviously you haven't!"

"I mean it's as if it had happened to someone else."

"You don't love Miss Maria Wakhelyana at all, Mister Ghichka?"

"I love you, sweetheart. I love you—period."

"So do I, Mister Ghichka! I love you, period. I have only ever loved you, period. I shall never love anyone else, period."

We did something in that hayloft. We did something that Cendrella had never done with anyone before. And I did it, too, as though I had never done it. I did it as I had never done it, and, in truth, it was the first time.

"Good heavens, Mister Ghichka, if my father found out! He'd whip the skin off my back!"

"Fathers always say that, my sweetheart—what else can they say? But their heart thinks the opposite. Hearts love love, that's their job."

"The thing is . . . he does not love you the way I do."

"I should hope not, my sweetheart, I should hope not."

"He says . . . he says . . . "

"Go ahead! I'm not afraid of words: I've heard too many of them. What does he say?"

"No."

"Yes! Do you want me to tell you instead?"

"He says that you're a good-for-nothing and that you live on Mister Karl's charity . . . "

"That's true, in a way. But I am good for loving you. I am sure that if he knew that—"

"Oh, no! Never! Never! I would rather kill myself!"

The days rolled on. And the nights, when love was so strong it became like pain, like an obstacle to living.

Not long ago I went to see Karl after his performance. He was haggard, drained. His troubled eyes settled on things without seeing them. The farmer had thrown a towel across his shoulders. His wife was rubbing off the rouge he wore so that his features would stand out even for spectators at the back of the room. He sat inertly between them, idly cradling a goblet of cider in his fingers.

"Karl!" I said. "You were magnificent! How are you feeling, old friend?"

He turned toward me like a punch-drunk boxer.

"But he can hardly stay upright!" I exclaimed. "This monkey is dying of exhaustion! He's going to have to stop! He needs rest! A vacation! This can't go on! He'll collapse!"

Did I dream it, or did my old friend give me a grateful smile? I did not have time to find out. I had scarcely ended my little speech before our host had me by the scruff of the neck and was dragging me out into the yard.

"Now you listen to me," he said. "I'm a patient man, but there are limits. You're going to stop seeing my monkey, right now! Can't you see that all your weeping and wailing is upsetting him? Are you trying to undermine his morale? I'm warning you, if you ruin this animal, I'm going to kick you both out! And right after that I'll be on the telephone to Krazkoch! It seems a monkey escaped from the Kirchenstahl Garden there last spring, taking the cash register with him, and the municipality has put a price on his head. Distinguishing marks: straw hat and malacca cane. Mean anything to you? They can't wait to cut him up in little bits! And now that we're on the subject — since you seem to need to have everything spelled out for you — stop creeping around my daughter because if you ever lay a finger on her, you bottom-of-the-barrel Lothario, with your dirty little good-for-nothing hands, I swear on my mother's bones that I'll kill you both like dogs! I won't have shame in this family, mister, and you can stake your life on that! Now about face and get back to your quarters, my little gentleman, on the double! And have a good time there because tomorrow I'm putting you and all your belongings in the stable. And count yourself lucky that that's all I'm going to do for now!"

That was that. I went up to my room without seeing either my friend or fair Cendrella, even though I loved her more than the night loves stars.

I packed my things. But I wasn't going to the stables. I was leaving for good. They had seen the last of me.

I left the hat and cane in full view on the bed. Karl might need them.

And what could I leave for you, my sweetheart? I could leave me, the best of myself; all I would take would be my bag of bones and skin — not much really, not much more than a change of clothing.

I realized it now. I had been the ruin of everyone I had loved. My whole life had had no other purpose.

I had worshiped Miss Maria Wakhelyana. "You have stolen my golden years!" she had shouted. "You have ruined my life!" And what could I have said in denial?

I had had the best friend a man could ever have on this earth; I had happily sent him to his death.

And even my sister, when you think about it: Would

she have fallen victim to a dairy truck that did not have one chance in a million of jumping the curb unless the tenderness I had felt for her had not been a form of curse?

But it was all over. The blinkers had fallen from my eyes. I would no longer be a blind weapon in destiny's hand. Karl, Cendrella, I will save you from my murderous love! This time I will vanquish those cackling demons who toy with our hearts and our lives the way we roll dice on bar counters.

I stole down the stairs. The key was always over the door, Cendrella had told me. I opened the door silently. The dog recognized me and did not bark. I detached the sidecar from the motorcycle; it would have been selfish to take both parts of the vehicle: Karl, too, might want to escape one of these days. I did not start the engine until I had left the last house behind me.

It was a broad and beautiful January night with a full moon. The snow-covered fields shimmered like lakes in sunlight, like silver plates. Nothing moved. The silence was an immense musical note, overflowing the universe and seeming to roll ever outward to the final consummation of the centuries.

It was so cold that the skin of my face stretched tight over my bones and became as hard and as stiff as a metal mask.

Through the film of ice carpeting the road, I could see round pebbles the color of irises, like treasures petrified in the rivers of time.

What did they understand of all this? Yet what else did they need to understand if it was not the small, eternal beauty of a pebble rolling aimlessly across the surface of a world that cannot even remember how it lost its memory? I will tell you what was happening. I will explain everything. It was nothing. A trifle. It was Ghichka Pik-topek taking his leave.

Watch. He straddles his motorbike. He fiddles with a brake lever and turns a handle. He kicks at the starter. Nothing. Bad weather for motorbikes. Splendid weather for disappearing into the blue! He kicks again. He kicks yet again. And again. And again. He is not worried. He knows he has to leave. Leave. Far away. Far away. Even farther. Come on, one more kick. There, that did it! She's turning over. What did I tell you? Ghichka Piktopek, the man who destroys everything he loves, dirty Ghichka, bad-luck Ghichka, is off.

At first I rode carefully. Ice. The wheelbarrow wheel in front. The counterweight of the sidecar, no longer there. Then, to hell with it all! I was afraid of nothing, I was already dead! Twist the throttle. Flat out! Pierced by thousands of tiny needles, I flew through the night wind. My hair stood straight and stiff on my scalp like a crown of thorns. Faster, faster! I screamed my agony to the stars . . .

When I opened my eyes, I was truly dead. Above my head were the branches of a tree.

How lucky the dead are! They see the world the way lovers see it. But no, I couldn't be dead, for here was my motorbike beside me. Or what was left of it. Don't tell me they bury motorbikes as well—not in the state this one was in, anyway!

It and I were lying in strange postures at the bottom of a deep ditch on a palanquin of ice that crackled when I moved. And it was already dawn.

I clearly saw each blade of grass. They were white and red, but, because of the frost, they looked as if they had been cast in bronze. One of them had pierced my side. It hurt. I had to pull it out.

But it was not a blade of grass. No. Do you know what it was? It was the piece of mirror bearing the imprint of my friend's face. And do you know what? You'll never guess. It was unbroken! I knew its shape by heart: It had lost not a single splinter.

Dear mirror! My last consolation. The irrefutable proof that once I had lived.

But how strange! Could it be a hallucination? No. I can see it with the same clarity, the same impartiality as all the rest. The person looking at me from this piece of glass treated to reflect images is indeed my friend—but alive!

His eyes are glowing. His mouth is open in a friendly smile. He is going to speak! He is about to tell me a secret, I feel it in every fiber of my being. He is about to reveal to me the meaning of everything I have so far gropingly accomplished, without ever being certain that I wasn't doing the opposite of what I thought I was doing.

He is going to tell me the secret of love, how to love so that love harms no one, endangers no one, forces no one to set off across the countryside in the middle of the night, his heart in shreds . . .

I do not know what happened. Doubtless I was too excited. Too overwhelmed. I dropped the mirror. It fell only from my hands to my breast, a few inches at most. But it shattered like a clay pipe in a shooting gallery at a country fair.

I would never learn the secret of love. Nothing remained of my life. A few glass splinters. The carcass of a motorcycle. The broken body of a man whose spirit was desperately clutching at memories fleeing like rats swarming off a sinking ship.

Cendrella, my love fragile as evening light. Karl, poor dear old Karl, whose life was and will be nothing but the illusion of a million lives a million times less necessary than your own . . . And you, my friend, the stranger I accosted one morning at the crossroads of my poor destiny: "Excuse me, sir, excuse me, but do you recognize me?" You who roared with laughter over the small pleasures of life and who gave Miss Maria Wakhelyana the only love worthy of her. You who bought me a cap too big for me, believing I was as big as you . . . You who brought me a new present every time . . . Oh, those little packages, Benazar Folykhulo (you see, I can even say your name now). Did I ever thank you enough for your little packages? Was I able to tell you, my friend? Was I able to say enough . . .

My eyes grow dim. I feel nothing. But, yes, I sense someone coming. Someone is walking on the frozen grass beside me! Lord God! Almighty Lord! Who is there? Karl! Karl! It's you! You followed me! You found me! My Karl! You! You!

He looks at me. His face is close to mine once more. His eyes brilliant with tears. Karl! I knew it!

But what is this, Karl, what is this? A present? For me? You shouldn't have! Oh, a little white box with a fine red ribbon! Undo it, Karl! Undo it for me, old friend, please, you've already done so much for me!

Oh! Oh! God who sees everything, see this before I fall asleep.

It is cracked. It is not new. But it is a doorknob.